BILL DOYLE

CRIME THROUGH TIME™

NABBED!

THE 1925 JOURNAL OF G. CODD FITZMORGAN

LITTLE, BROWN AND COMPANY

New York Boston London

Cover illustration by Steve Cieslawski
Interior illustrations by Anthony Lewis
Back cover and title page illustration by Brian Dow
Photos: pp. 22, 31/Ablestock; pp. 30, 106/Library of Congress; p. 120/
TTB/U.S. Department of the Treasury
The Inspector photos: p. 1, Zuma Press/KPA/Newscom (top); p. 1 (bottom), pp. 2–4 (all photos), Library of Congress

Developed by Nancy Hall, Inc.

Little, Brown and Company

Time Warner Book Group
1271 Avenue of the Americas, New York, NY 10020
Visit our Web site at www.lb-kids.com

First Edition: March 2006

Library of Congress Cataloging-in-Publication Data

Doyle, Bill H., 1968-
Nabbed! 1925 : the journal of G. Codd Fitzmorgan / by Bill Doyle.—1st ed.
p. cm. — (Crime through time)
Summary: In 1925, fourteen-year-old amateur detective G. Codd Fitzmorgan finds himself at a lavish party in a storm-battered island mansion, embroiled in a mystery involving a séance, a missing aviator, and the sale of liquor banned under Prohibition.
ISBN 0-316-05737-1 (trade pbk. : alk. paper)
[1. Prohibition—Fiction. 2. Aeronautics—History—Fiction. 3. North Carolina—History—20th century—Fiction. 4. Mystery and detective stories.] I. Title. II. Series: Doyle, Bill H., 1968- Crime through time.
PZ7.D7725Nab 2006
[Fic]—dc22 2005018600

10 9 8 7 6 5 4 3 2 1

Printed in the United States of America

ACKNOWLEDGMENTS

A thank-you of historic proportions to Nancy Hall for making this book and the Crime Through Time series a reality. To Kirsten Hall, for her keen editing and insightful grasp of the overall picture, and to Atif Toor for making the whole book come alive visually.

Special thanks to the editors at Little, Brown: Andrea Spooner, Jennifer Hunt, and Phoebe Sorkin, who are always dead-on, always incisive, and never discouraging. And thanks to Riccardo Salmona for his constant support.

Waves are huge! Crew running
to. frightened
I am on deck of ferry. Water everywhere
No land in sight.
Is this my last journal entry?
"There it is!" A deckhand shouted.
He's right. I can see the dim
outline through the fog — Hunter Island

June 12, 1925

8:50 PM

We made it to Hunter Island!

I guess I overreacted to the rough seas. I actually ripped out the previous entry so no one could ever read how scared I was. But a great detective learns to deal with all the facts, both good and bad—so I taped it back in.

Who knew a ferry ride could be so terrifying? Crossing to the island from the coast of North Carolina, the storm hammered us with rain and whipping winds. Monstrous waves swept over the deck as if they might swallow the boat whole.

Somehow, we arrived safe and sound.

Gratefully, I stepped onto the dock and got my first close look at the Hatherford mansion. I gaped up in awe at the four-story home, which loomed over one end of the island like a massive, creepy castle. As long as two football fields, it sprouted in all directions with towers, chimneys, and gargoyles. According to reports, the mansion was full of secret passageways and hidden rooms!

The Hatherford mansion—quite impressive!

June 12, 1925

The ferry passengers were met by butlers and maids standing with open umbrellas. A stern-faced bald man wearing a starched butler's uniform walked over to me. "I am Charles," he said in a deep, rumbling voice. "I will show you to your room. Your bag will be brought up shortly."

"I'm G. Codd Fitzmorgan. Nice to meet you." I stuck out my hand. Charles shook it coldly and moved quickly away from the dock.

I had to rush to keep up. As we climbed a steep grassy incline in the lashing rain, I had the oddest feeling that the mansion's windows were like eyes. And that they were watching me.

"This way, please," Charles instructed, snapping me out of my eerie thoughts. We walked through ornately carved wood doors and into the house. I followed the butler through a shadowy front hall, up a long staircase made of black stone, and down a hallway lined with ancient suits of armor. After three more hallways and two staircases, I felt like I'd stepped into a fairy tale. "Should I leave a trail of bread crumbs?" I joked.

Charles didn't laugh. "With parents such as yours, I imagine you shouldn't have a problem detecting your way around."

So he had heard of my mom and dad. That isn't so strange. My parents are famous detectives who have cracked cases all around the world, from recovering a

dnapped panda in China to breaking up a counterfeiting ng here in the United States. They'd be here right now, ıt they're off solving their latest case—which is very ush-hush. I think it has something to do with the overnment of Siam, but I'm not sure.

As Charles and I continued walking, I saw other uests being led into their rooms. Yet we traveled on and n. Finally, Charles stopped and swung open a heavy wood oor. At first, I thought he was showing me into a grand all or a ballroom.

"This is my room?" I asked, my eyes running about the ammoth space.

"Oh, yes," Charles said with a touch of disapproval. It does seem like a lot for a child..."

A child? "I'm fourteen," I said, a little too defensively.

But he was right. This was a lot of space for anyone, hild or not. There was a four-poster bed, a gigantic replace with a roaring fire, and a rolltop desk (where I m writing now) big enough for five people to sit at. It was uch cheerier than the other parts of the house I'd seen.

My room must be the biggest in the house!

June 12, 1925

I walked over to one of the three floor-to-ceiling windows. I had an amazing view of the airplane landing strip. Beyond that, I could see a group of trees, the ferry dock, and the churning sea. There was no sign of the boat that had brought us to the island.

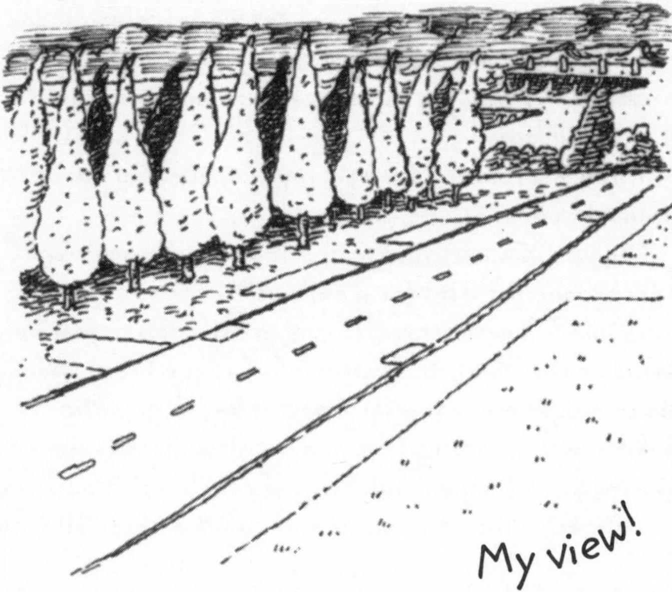

"Where's the ferry?" I asked Charles, who was adding another log to the fire.

"The crew took it back to the mainland," he answered. "The dock here offers little protection during storm conditions. And the seas will only be getting worse."

"Worse?" That didn't seem possible. From where I stood, it looked like the rolling waves had tripled in size since we arrived.

Charles's lips bent into a thin smile. "Just last summer, we were without the ferry for four days during one storm."

If this was supposed to scare me, it didn't.

"What a fantastic place to be stranded!" I said, glancing around the room again. "Do the other eighty weekend guests have rooms like mine?"

"No, this is one of the finest," Charles said, closing the fireplace screen. "Miss Pinkerton informed the staff she will be keeping an eye on you this weekend and wanted to make you comfortable. She requested you be given this room."

Judge always spoils me. One year, she hired actors to come to my backyard and reenact an unsolved bank robbery that had taken place in Tulsa, Oklahoma. She timed me while I cracked the case. Another year, Judge took me to see my idol, the magician Harry Houdini—and then backstage to meet him! Whenever she's around, amazing things happen.

But where was she now? "Judge wasn't on the ferry," I said. "And I haven't seen—"

"Who?" Charles interrupted, clearly having no idea who I was talking about.

"Right. Sorry. I mean Miss Pinkerton," I said. "Justine Pinkerton. Everyone in my family calls her Judge."

"Oh?" Charles asked. But I could tell he really meant, "And why on earth would you do that?"

I almost told him that I've often wondered the same thing. Once I asked my mom that very question. "She wants to go to law school, but she's not a real judge," I had said. "So why do you call her that?" My mom just

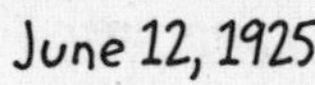

WHAT IN THE WORD?

PRIVATE EYE: A term meaning detective, derived from the logo of the Pinkerton Detective Agency. Allan Pinkerton opened the first national detective organization in 1850. Its logo was an open eye with the slogan "We Never Sleep." Pinkerton foiled an assassination attempt on Abraham Lincoln, cracked countless cases, and specialized in railroad security. He wrote a series of 18 books about his life that made him a true celebrity. The open eye trademark was linked with detective work—so people started calling all detectives "private eyes."

Judge is a Pinkerton.

laughed and said, "One day I think you'll figure that out for yourself." All I know is that Judge is from a famous family of detectives.

But I didn't say any of that to Charles. Instead, I just shrugged. Charles gave me a tiny smile. "Miss Pinkerton is arranging last-minute details for the party."

That made sense. After all, the party is the reason we're all here. Judge is head over heels in love with the famous test pilot John Hatherford. They're getting married in August, and we're celebrating their engagement this weekend.

Charles handed me an envelope. "She asked me to give you this. Please let me know if you need anything." Before I could thank him, he turned and left the room.

June 12, 1925

I sat down at the desk and ripped open the envelope, eager to read the message from Judge. Here's what it said:

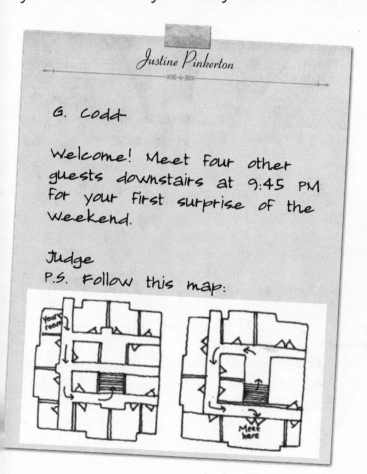

Justine Pinkerton

G. Codd

Welcome! Meet four other guests downstairs at 9:45 PM for your first surprise of the weekend.

Judge

P.S. Follow this map:

Your room

Meet here

Leave it to Judge. This weekend is supposed to be for her—and she's the one handing out surprises. I can't wait to change into my tuxedo and see what she has in store for me!

Virgil Gates
Asyla Notabe
Mr. and Mrs. Kartier

June 12, 1925

9:45 PM

After one or two wrong turns in the confusing hallways of the mansion, I finally arrived at the spot marked on the map.

Right away, I recognized the four people already waiting in the hall outside the parlor. I had seen them on the ferry ride over.

There was the nervous, twitchy businessman named Virgil Gates. He had spent most of the boat trip with his head over the rail, feeding his lunch to the fish. At the moment, Virgil was gazing adoringly at his gorgeous girlfriend, Asyla Notabe, who wore a dress made of long, sparkly silver tassels. Asyla leaned her perfectly sculpted back against the wall, looking bored and stroking her long black hair as if it were a cat. An elderly couple, Mr. and Mrs. Kartier, were dressed like royalty. Mrs. Kartier wore a tiara in her silver hair, and Mr. Kartier had a kingly red sash across his tuxedo jacket.

Before I could say hello to anyone, a raspy voice called from the shadows of a nearby parlor.

"Enter! All who vish to speak vith ze dead, come and enter!"

Who could resist an invitation like that? The five of us stepped into the darkened room. Once we were inside, the oak door slammed shut with a bang, and Virgil Gates cried out.

"What a sap!" Asyla hissed and pushed past him, sauntering like a film star. She was probably the most

Beautiful Asyla

beautiful woman I had ever seen.

I had heard about Asyla from the society pages and from my parents. They'd first met her years ago on a train trip across the United States. After that, Asyla's life had been one long streak of bad luck. When Asyla was a teenager, her mom was sent to prison. She later escaped and went into hiding, without Asyla. No other family members had come forward to claim her, so Asyla had been raised in an orphanage in Chicago. That's why my parents were so curious about how Asyla was now able to afford to travel in such high style. They had heard rumors that her mom had started a new life of crime and was secretly sending Asyla money.

Now I was meeting her in person!

Our little group gathered around a large table in the center of the room, which was crowded with antique furniture. The flame of a single candle cast sinister shadows on our faces. And a large crystal ball shone dully, resting on a brass stand next to a violin.

Asyla was to my right. To my left, Mrs. Kartier gripped her husband's arm and made squeaking sounds like a frightened chipmunk.

That's just what Judge wanted...for us to be scared. It was a perfect night for a séance, I thought. Lightning flashed on gargoyles, making them look alive as they peered through the windows.

June 12, 1925

SANDRA'S SCHOOL OF SÉANCE

CONTACTING THE DEAD

IS YOUR PARTY DEAD? LIVEN IT UP WITH A SÉANCE!

SÉANCE:
A gathering to call a spirit with the guidance of a medium. (*Séance* comes from the French word for sitting or meeting.)

MEDIUM:
Master of the séance, sometimes called a spiritualist. This person is in charge of calling and communicating with the spirits of people who have died.

SITTERS:
Guests at the table.

PSYCHIC ENERGY:
Sitters touch the little fingers of each hand to those of the people on either side or simply hold hands. This will boost the energy needed to summon spirits.

TABLE TURNING:
Spirits may answer questions by knocking, pounding, or moving the table. (Abraham Lincoln and Sir Arthur Conan Doyle were interested in table turning!)

DIM LIGHT:
Darkness helps the medium and the sitters focus.

Judge got the idea for a séance from this ad.

June 12, 1925

Then, across the wood table, a man stepped into the dim light of the candle, and I knew at a glance we were in for a letdown.

"I am Mang ze Magnifico!" the tall man announced in what sounded like a French accent by way of New York. He had a long black beard and wore a purple cape emblazoned with gold stars and moons.

I guess for dramatic effect, Mang began flapping his arms wildly to make the cape ripple up and down. This only made him look like a deranged bat—and sent dust flying off his blue tuxedo.

Mang ze not-so-

Virgil Gates waved the air before his thin, pointy nose. "Allergies! Allergies!" he cried between massive sneezes.

Sweeping back her long hair, Asyla Notabe giggled merrily. Like a queen amused by a jester, she pointed at Mang's slightly tattered outfit. "Mr. Magnifico, you might want to contact a good tailor rather than the dead." I felt my heart skip a beat as Asyla turned to me and asked, "Am I right or what?"

She was talking to me! Excited, I opened my mouth to answer her. But something sparked in Asyla's eyes. "Why am I asking you, Fitzmorgan?" She spat out my name as if it were disgusting and turned away.

My face burned from her unexpected hostility. I said, "Excuse me—"

June 12, 1925

Mang interrupted me. He was glaring at Asyla. "Laughter? You produce ze laughter? What I do is deadly serious!" Mang flapped his arms again and bellowed, "I am a spiritualist!"

For a second, Asyla stared at Mang and then burst out laughing. "Oh, dry up, vould you?" Asyla said, mocking Mang's accent.

While Asyla's giggles and Virgil's sneezes filled the room, Mang dragged over a small square table. He held up his right hand to show us that he was not concealing anything in his palm.

"Vitness my power!" he shouted and brought his palm down on the flat surface of the small table with a smack. Mang's eyes rolled into the back of his head. He lifted his hand and the table rose with it—as if the wood and his skin had magically fused together.

Asyla gasped, Virgil stopped sneezing, and Mr. and Mrs. Kartier appeared to have stopped breathing.

Child's play, I thought.

I had hoped Mang would prove to be more of a challenge. I wanted to try out the detective skills I'd learned from studying Houdini.

HOW TO FOOL SITTERS AT A SÉANCE

TABLE LIFTING

- Find an old table—make sure it's small, light, and no one wants it anymore.
- Hammer a nail with a small head into the top of table.
- Put a loose ring on a finger and slide your hand along the surface until the ring slides over the head of the nail. (It might help to cut a slot into the ring.)
- Keep your hand flat on the table surface and lift it from the floor.

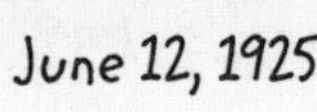

I wrote a letter to
Houdini, and this is
got back. It's just a
letter probably writ
his secretary, but I
carry it with me.

HOUDINI

278 WEST 113TH STREET
NEW YORK, N. Y.

Dear Fan,

Thank you for your interest in my life. Here are a few facts you might not know.

I was born Ehrich Weiss in Hungary in 1874. Four years later, my family moved to Wisconsin. I tried working as a trapeze artist but later turned to magic. I read a book by Jean Eugene Robert-Houdin, an amazing French magician from the 1800s. He was the first one to use real science in his act—something I wanted to do. In honor of him, I changed my name to Harry Houdini.

I'm the most famous magician in the world today. But that's not all I do. I've starred in silent movies. And lately, I've worked hard against fake mediums and phony mind readers who give illusionists like me a bad name. I attend séances disguised in a fake beard and eyeglasses. I've become an expert at detecting the hidden motions of the medium's hands, feet, and body that would produce the sounds and actions of spirits. I shine a light during the séance to show the sitters the trick. I then tear off my disguise and reveal myself as the great Houdini!

In fact, I'm not looking for fakes, but for a medium who can do what he or she claims.

Yours in magic,

Houdini

June 12, 1925

Mang lowered the small table to the floor with a flourish. In a stern voice, he told us that he would allow no further interruptions. He instructed us to sit at the large table and hold hands. Asyla took one of my hands and Mrs. Kartier took the other.

"Ve shall now contact ze dead!" Mang said. "Everyone watch ze ball of crystal and concentrate… concentrate!" The reflection of the candle burned in his eyes. "Now repeat after me, 'Join us, spirit of ze dead.'"

It was piffle, but we repeated, "Join us, spirit of the dead" over and over.

Mang threw his head back and shouted into the air, "Spirit! Spirit! Are you in ze room?" His head jerked back down. "Ah, yes, I feel it! I feel ze presence!"

Mang calling a spirit

Virgil's eyes bulged slightly. "How do you know?" he whispered fearfully.

"Is it my sister Estelle?" Mrs. Kartier said to Mang. "If it's Estelle, will you ask her where she hid the gold teakettle?"

Mang seemed annoyed by the questions and asked the air, "Are you Estelle? Lift the table twice if no!"

There was a pause, and just as the others started to relax, the table leaped up as if on its own. It did so once—and then again. Mrs. Kartier screamed. Blinding light exploded into the room as lightning crashed all around the mansion.

Mang smiled. "Very goodly. No, not Estelle. Zhank you, spirit, for clearing zat up—" He was interrupted as the violin suddenly skipped along the surface of the table and flew into the air, with the bow following after. Mrs. Kartier screamed again, and her husband joined her.

The instrument swung over our heads. Then the bow crashed into the strings of the violin and scraped across them, producing a sound like twelve cats in excruciating pain. And just as violently, the violin clattered back to the surface of the table and was still.

The violin played—badly!

"Ze spirit of ze famous French pirate Jean-Claude Noir iz here!" Mang announced. "And he has ze questions por one of you!"

June 12, 1925

With eyes burning brighter than ever, Mang shot out his index finger and pointed it at Virgil. "You!" Mang boomed. "Ze spirit has ze questions por vous, Mr. Virgil Gates."

Asyla inched away from Virgil, who looked ready to run screaming from the room. "For me?" He squeaked.

"Yes!" Mang said. "He vants to know vhat it iz you are doing here in ze mansion!"

These words seemed to push Virgil closer to some kind of attack.

Virgil

Enough was enough. Judge wouldn't want this. The séance had gone way beyond fun entertainment.

"These people are terrified," I said to Mang.

Mang was furious at the interruption. "Silence!" he hissed.

I kept my eyes on Virgil, pointing at Mang. "This man is an illusionist—"

"I am not! I am a spiritualist!" Mang screamed. "I demand silence!"

"—and not a very talented illusionist, either," I continued, ignoring him.

Like a drowning man grasping at a lifeline, Virgil grabbed at my words. "But the spirit..."

"A spirit didn't do anything. It was all Mang." I hated to ruin a fellow magician's act. But Mang was giving all illusionists a bad name by scaring these people.

Virgil's eyes started to lose their panicked glow. "The table! How did it leap up on its own? Mang was holding hands with us..."

"He could have moved the table with his legs." I demonstrated by jamming my thighs up against the table. It jumped slightly.

"Ach! Ze insults ze child heaps upon me!" Mang cried.

But Virgil was listening to me. His face wasn't nearly as red, and I could see he was embarrassed to have caused a scene in front of Asyla. "And what about the violin?" he asked.

"The violin is controlled by wires, I'm certain," I said. "If there were lights in this room, you'd see them. Holding hands keeps the sitters from reaching out in the darkness and discovering hidden wires, which Mang controls with his leg."

Your very own
AUTHENTIC
CRYSTAL
BALL!
Gaze into the future!
Amaze your friends!
ONLY $1.99
plus tax

Too bad they don't work!

This time Mang didn't protest. He just kept glaring at me.

"And this." I picked up the heavy crystal ball from its stand. "This is just a big ball of —"

Lightning flashed. Then I saw it. My mouth snapped shut.

"Big ball of what?" Virgil whined, growing anxious again.

Asyla noticed my frozen stare. "What's eating you?"

But I couldn't speak. In the flash of lightning I had spotted something in the corner of the parlor. Something that made my blood run cold.

A shadowy figure had been standing there. Its hand had reached out—then with a blue flash, the strange ghostlike shape vanished.

June 12, 1925

By the time the others followed my gaze, the figure was gone.

I could explain a lot. A moving table, a floating violin, mysterious messages from the grave—but this...this was something no illusionist I'd ever encountered could create. The figure I spotted had simply disappeared into thin air. Was this a spirit after all?

Virgil was saved!

The shock took a moment to set in. Suddenly I jerked backward. I toppled over in my chair. The crystal ball I'd been holding shot up into the air, high over Virgil's head. He was too panicked to move. The crystal ball arced...it was about to crash down on top of Virgil's skull—

When two hands shot out and snatched the crystal ball out of the air.

"There's a difference between using this ball to contact the spirits and using it to join them," a voice said. I instantly felt better.

Standing over me was a glamorous woman who stood nearly six feet tall in high heels. Her blond hair was cut in a fashionable bob, and she wore a sleeveless dress covered with glittering purple rhinestones.

It was Judge!

Holding the crystal ball, she peered down at me, where I still lay on my back on the floor. "G. Codd, what is it?"

"I thought...," I stammered, taking her outstretched hand and climbing to my feet.

"What? Tell me." Judge's green eyes were full of concern.

When I didn't answer her, I watched Judge do what she does best. She took charge of the situation.

She put the crystal ball back in its stand and turned her attention to Mang. "What's going on? I hired you to show the guests a good time, not shock them into a stupor."

Mang shrugged sheepishly and seemed to wither under her gaze.

It sounds ridiculous, but I was shaking. "I saw someone...something...in the corner."

This is where the figure vanished.

June 12, 1925

Judge looked at me. Her face softened as she said, "Not to worry, my friend."

The rhinestones on her dress clicked as Judge strode to the wall and flipped a switch. The room was suddenly ablaze with the light from two mammoth crystal chandeliers. Judge pulled on the velvet cord to call the butler as Mang scurried about tucking wires beneath his cape. But I was no longer interested in him. I had seen something, something that could not have been created by moving knees and thin wire.

"Come over here, G. Codd, and let's see what we can see," she said. She was standing in the corner where I had seen a figure. I could see her sharp eyes running over everything, trying to detect something suspicious. "Nothing's here. Just a pile of presents for my engagement party."

Charles rushed into the room, a smile on his face showing he was eager to help.

"Why on earth are these presents in here?" Judge asked him.

The butler's smiled disappeared. He looked terrified of Judge. She can have that effect on people—without even realizing it.

"I am so sorry, Miss Pinkerton," Charles stammered. "The parlor maid found a large crate near the cellar door and brought it and the others in here."

"Someone should tell our Miss Pinkerton that it's tacky to argue with the help," Asyla whispered loudly to Virgil. He chuckled as if she were the epitome of humor, and the two left the room.

Judge ignored them. "It's fine, Charles," she said,

some of the familiar lilt back in her voice. "Would you take them up to my room when you have a moment, please?"

Charles picked up as many of the packages as he could carry and left the room.

Mang had packed up his things and made a hasty exit with the Kartiers.

Judge must have seen I still had a case of the heebie-jeebies. She stepped closer and rested a hand on my shoulder. "Remember a few years ago when we talked about Occam's razor? Maybe that philosophy can help you now."

There were two explanations for the vanishing figure in the corner: It was a ghost of a long-dead pirate called Jean-Claude Noir or it was just a trick of the light. I wasn't completely out of my mind—so it was obvious which explanation was the simplest.

OCCAM'S RAZOR

William of Occam was a master of logic from the Middle Ages who wrote, "Pluralitas non est ponenda sine neccesitate." His Latin translates roughly as: Of two competing theories of explanations, all other things being equal, the simpler one is preferred.

That means: Don't make life more complicated than it needs to be. Most of the time, the simple answer is the right one.

"G. Codd, you've got one of the best young detective minds I know. I trust in your ability to see through illusion. You should do the same." She gave my combed hair a good tussle. "Sorry about your surprise. I know Houdini's a hero of yours. This séance was supposed to be something you'd remember from this weekend."

"Thanks, Judge," I said. My heartbeat had slowed from its breakneck pace. Maybe Occam's razor was a form of denial, but it did make me feel better. I smiled at her. "And don't worry. I don't think I'll forget this night anytime soon."

"Bully for you!" Judge grinned. She took my arm and led me toward the door. "Now come on," she cried. "I'm so excited about my future with John. And I want us to have fun at the party!"

As we left the parlor, I made myself happy for Judge. But I couldn't shake the feeling that what I had seen was more than a trick of the light.

The Great Hall

June 12, 1925

11:10 PM

Big. Enormous. Of gargantuan proportions. Take these descriptions, multiply them by 1,000. That's one way to get an idea about the size of the mansion's Great Hall.

With a 40-foot-high ceiling, the Hall was easily large enough to house my father's 65-foot yacht—and then some. It was big enough for at least six basketball courts, and the three fireplaces were each large enough to hold a new Rolls-Royce.

Besides being the largest private room I had ever seen, the Great Hall had another unique feature. There was only one small window in the far wall. It was 10 inches wide by 8 inches tall.

Judge told me that the Hatherfords had bought the mansion two years ago from the previous owner—an infamous rumrunner. That's a person who transports liquor, which is highly illegal. In fact, the Great Hall had been a speakeasy at one point. The lack of windows prevented prying eyes from peering in.

Judge's fiancé,

BOOTLEGGERS, BEWARE!

As of 1920, the United States government will not stand for any violations of the 18th Amendment to the United States Constitution. This amendment prohibits the "manufacture, sale, or transportation of intoxicating liquors."

Yes, bootlegging—or smuggling liquor—may appear to be profitable. Al Capone is said to have made tens of millions in profits from his illegal business. But we will catch you sooner or later—and you will go to jail!

John Hatherford, had discovered that the mansion was riddled with secret passages, hiding places, and concealed doors. Judge said when John finally got the time to show her a few, she would tell me their locations. I'd get to explore them, too.

In the meantime, though, we had a party to explore. Judge and I stood at the top of the huge, 18-foot-wide staircase, looking down into the mansion's Great Hall. These stairs were one of just two ways in and out of the Great Hall—the other was a set of double doors that opened onto the side lawn.

If I had ever wondered why they call our decade the "Roaring Twenties," what I saw below would've put an end to that mystery. The Great Hall was a mass of swirling, glittering, sweating, eating, laughing guests. The engagement party had hit full steam!

Flappers surrounded the stage where a hot jazz band played "Lady, Be Good." The electric bulbs overhead had been dimmed, and the four blazing fires gave off an orange glow. Legs and arms flew everywhere as dancers struggled with the latest steps. A group of young girls

GERTIE'S GOSSIP PAGE

RUDOLPH RUMORS RUN RAMPANT!

Sources say the famous silent movie actor Rudolph Valentino was spotted entering a speakeasy. These gathering places serve illegal liquor and are called speakeasies because visitors must speak easy, or talk softly, once inside in order not to draw the attention of the police. Usually a visitor must whisper a secret password to gain entry. Gertie can only guess Rudy's password was "Mr. Romance."

How they came up with the word "speakeasy"

DANCE THE CHARLESTON IN STYLE!

For the latest in evening wear, look for flapper dresses that…

- are sleeveless
- have low necklines
- have dropped wastlines
- reveal ankles and calves
- are made of material that "floats"
- are heavily beaded or fringed

Add a long string of beads for a nice finishing touch!

with feathers in their hair burst into hysterical laughter trying to teach the Kartiers how to do the Charleston.

A man with slicked-back hair and a full-length fur coat spotted Judge. He pointed up at her and shouted, "It's the bride-to-be!" Soon others were calling out: "There she is!" and "Congratulations!" The excitement rippled across the room until it reached the jazz band. The lead horn player switched his tune to "Here Comes the Bride," and the rest of the band joined in.

With a wink at me, Judge gave the crowd a little bow. They shouted and clapped even louder.

As we headed down the stairs, Judge took my hand. She said softly to me, "After my mom and dad died, you and your parents became even more important to me." She gave my hand a squeeze. "I'm glad you're here, G. Codd. You're my family."

I smiled at Judge. She had a way of always making me feel special. We reached the bottom of the stairs, and arms reached out to greet her. Judge said, "G. Codd, make sure you eat something!" The crowd whisked her away.

June 12, 1925

Finding something to eat wasn't hard. Countless waiters spun in and out of groups of guests, balancing trays heaped with caviar, finger sandwiches of duck, and other delicacies. The servers were constantly refilling their trays at tables that dripped with succulent roasts, mounds of chocolates, and oceans of some strange-smelling punch. Towering over these tables were several sculptures carved from huge blocks of ice.

I walked over to look more closely at one of the ice sculptures. It was Judge! She was smiling and holding hands with her fiancé, John Hatherford. The artist had carved John in his pilot's uniform, leather fur-lined jacket, cap, and goggles.

I was struck by a familiar feeling of surprise. John is great. But I always thought Judge would end up with someone who enjoyed detective work—or encouraged her dreams of becoming a lawyer.

Even in melting ice, John was a handsome man with a mischievous, lopsided grin—the kind all the girls fall for. (I admit after I met him for the first time last year, I practiced that smile in the mirror. But I could never seem to get it quite right.)

The next ice sculpture showed the other love of John's life: JENNY.

JENNY was John's second single-engine plane. Eight months

JENNY, John's plane

ago, his first airplane had burst into flames for no clear reason over the North Carolina coast. He'd jumped out of the plane without a parachute and landed safely in the water. This earned him the nickname Jumpin' John.

John flew JENNY on trips for Hatherford Air Courier, Inc., the company that Judge ran. But picking up and dropping off packages wasn't enough. Jumpin' John was looking for new challenges. Dangerous challenges.

In fact, right now, John was soaring high over the Atlantic Ocean. About thirty hours ago, he had taken off from a field in France. He was due to arrive at the party by landing his plane on the small airstrip at the side of the house—becoming the first person ever to fly solo nonstop across the Atlantic!

AIRPLANE NEWS & GLOBAL REPORT

Competition for the Orteig Prize is hitting new heights! Several pilots have been killed or injured trying to win the prize, $25,000 offered by hotel owner Raymond Orteig to the first person who can fly nonstop between New York and Paris.

I was about to dig into another piece of cake when the jazz band stopped playing. All eyes in the room turned to watch as Mr. Hiram Hatherford, John's father, took the stage. Hiram Hatherford looked like he could have played football when he was younger. His face had grown a little wrinkled, but his chest was like a barrel and his neck was thicker than my thigh.

"Good evening, everyone!" Mr. Hatherford boomed. "Are you having fun?"

June 12, 1925

The guests shouted their appreciation. Mr. Hatherford waited for all the cheers to die down.

"During my long life," he told the crowd, "I have amassed great wealth. But nothing can compare to the treasure about to enter my family. The beautiful Justine Pinkerton and my son will soon be married!" After a burst of applause, Mr. Hatherford continued, "who knew four years ago that when I asked this brilliant woman to start and run our new air delivery service, I was 'hiring' a daughter-in-law? She has done amazing things with the business—"

Cutting in, Mr. Kartier said, "A lady should know her place!" There was general laughter from the guests.

"Hey, Frank," Mr. Hatherford told him, "join us in the '20s. Women can run businesses. Thank goodness, too. With Justine running the business, John can keep his head in the clouds. He flies deliveries all across the country. And he has a very special delivery to make tonight."

He paused and a woman in the crowd shouted, "What's he bringing us, Hiram?"

Mr. Hatherford laughed. "He's delivering his heart to Justine Pinkerton, by way of Europe." A mixture of sighs, groans, and cheers broke out. Mr. Hatherford went on, "As a special engagement present to Justine, John is going to be the first person to make a nonstop solo transatlantic flight tonight!" The Great Hall rang with applause as the guests clapped and cheered. Mr. Hatherford had to shout above the din to be heard. "Why don't we get Justine up here to say a few words—"

Mr. Hatherford was interrupted by a woman with

dozens of peacock feathers in her hair. She yelled at the top of her lungs, "There he is!"

The woman was pointing at the small window. People pushed and shoved to gather around the tiny pane of glass and watch a teeny airplane bump out of the stormy night sky. Someone dimmed the lights overhead, making the scene outside a little easier to see—which was a good thing because the window provided a pretty blurry view of the action.

Real peacock feathers!

"I can't see!" someone yelled and pushed in closer to the window. A few guests, including me, stood up on chairs to get a better look over the others' heads.

We watched the airplane's jerky progress. It was being buffeted by the high winds as if it were a toy. The miniscule figure of the pilot could now be seen. Finally, after a few tense moments, the silent, anxious crowd watched the plane hit the airstrip with a jolt and taxi down the runway.

Cheers exploded, filling the Great Hall with deafening excitement. The crowd rushed toward the double doors that led to the side lawn and the airstrip, but Charles blocked the exit.

Everyone crowded around the window.

"For goodness' sake, Charles, open the doors!" Mr. Hatherford called to the butler.

"But the rain, sir!" Charles called back. "It will ruin the carpets!"

Mr. Hatherford laughed. "Who cares about a little rain? These people want to welcome their hero!"

The butler threw open the doors. Cool night air swept into the room as guests poured out onto the patio. Judge and Mr. Hatherford led the way. My eyes went directly from the tiny window that showed the plane to the view through the double doors. I saw the plane sitting off in the distance, under a now-clearing sky. The rain had temporarily stopped.

I had to wait for the crowd to clear before I could fit out the double doors. Knowing this was a historic moment, I used the time to sketch the landing.

June 12, 1925

I stepped out in the night air. The wet grass instantly soaked through my shoes. The light of the moon illuminated the dramatic scene. But the only sound I heard was the pattering of water as it dripped from the eaves of the mansion.

The crowd was gathered around the plane. But there were no cheers. No shouts of congratulations. The flashbulbs of newspaper photographers remained dark.

Why aren't they cheering? I wondered. I walked closer, politely pushing my way through the crowd.

When I saw the plane, I understood.

Judge was staring at the cockpit with confusion and fear on her face.

"Where is he?" Mr. Hatherford shouted. "Where is my son?"

Judge took his hand and answered, "He isn't here."

I gazed long and hard inside the small, battered plane. It was completely empty. There was no sign of the pilot.

Jumpin' John Hatherford had vanished.

Mr. Hatherford collapsed.

June 13, 1925

12:00 Midnight

"John! Johnny!" Mr. Hatherford's voice cracked as he shouted his son's name. Stunned, the crowd watched in silence as the big man banged on the side of the plane. "John, come out of there right now."

He broke off. The reality of the situation registered on his ruddy face. There was not a living soul on board that airplane. But how could that be? I had watched the plane land myself. My eyes had gone directly from the Great Hall window to the door—they had not left sight of the plane long enough for someone to sneak away.

Mr. Hatherford seemed to be thinking the same thing. He turned to look at us, as if searching for someone in the crowd who was pulling a prank. "Airplanes cannot land by themselves! He must be on board! This isn't funny. I want whoever is involved in this to stop it, right now. John, this is not a game—"

Mr. Hatherford's words broke off again—his face crumpled in pain as he collapsed against the plane. One hand flew to his chest then grasped his left arm. Was he having a heart attack?

Judge sprang into action. She touched his shoulder. "Hiram, breathe deeply."

"This...is...not...funny...," he wheezed.

"Just breathe," Judge told Mr. Hatherford in a soothing voice. "You must come with me, Hiram." Still bracing John's dad, Judge leaned in close to me. "G. Codd, I have to take Mr. Hatherford back to the house. The police will not be able to arrive until the stormy seas die down. In the meantime, I need you to help me. Do you know what to do?"

It took me a moment to realize what she meant. "You want me to start the investigation?"

"Yes," she answered. Her bright eyes scanned the area, probably looking for signs of foul play. "I hope this will turn out to be a joke, and John will show up at any moment, but I'm not sure..."

"Not to worry," I told her. "I know exactly what to do." That might have been overstating things, but I wanted to comfort her.

She gave me a nod that said "Then get to it!" and led Mr. Hatherford back to the house.

Now it was my turn for action. Careful not to disturb any possible evidence, I moved in front of the cockpit door so the guests gathered around could all see me. "Ladies and gentlemen!" I called out. "We need to close off this area. We have a missing person and a possible kidnapping. Right now, you could be trampling evidence we'll need to find John Hatherford!"

No one was listening. Guests were chattering away, throwing out wild speculations about what might have happened to John. Mrs. Kartier was talking about creatures from Mars.

I shouted, "Excuse me!" and whistled with two fingers like Judge had taught me years ago. But still, the crowd acted as if I wasn't even there.

Through my growing frustration, I spotted Asyla in the crowd. She was smiling so pleasantly I thought, Good, an ally!

But then she turned to the feathered woman. "He's only fourteen, you know," Asyla said loudly, pointing at me. "Just Fitz Morgan's child playacting as a grown-up."

If for some reason Asyla had wanted to discredit me, her words had the opposite effect. "Didn't that kid solve the mystery of that bank robbery in Tulsa, Oklahoma?" the woman next to Asyla asked. "His parents have cracked more cases than the Secret Service!" someone else commented.

A ripple of excitement ran through the crowd. Faces turned toward me and everyone stopped talking.

Suddenly, I had the entire crowd's attention.

I mouthed the words "thank you" to Asyla. The smile stayed on her face, yet her dark eyes had turned cold.

Everyone was looking at me.

June 13, 1925

TEC TIP

SO YOU WANT TO BE A DETECTIVE!

The crime scene includes the exact spot where the crime took place and areas from which the site can be entered or exited. Here's how to seal off a large crime scene:

1) Cordon off, or close, the crime scene using rope, large objects, or people

2) Only individuals who are absolutely necessary to working the scene are allowed in. Keep track of everyone who enters or leaves.

3) Watch out for nosy neighbors and members of the press—they have ways of gaining entry!

4) Walk through the area—careful not to disrupt evidence—and get a feel for how to approach the scene.

5) Document all evidence by keeping notes, drawing sketches, and taking photographs (if a camera is available).

What did she have against me? I wondered. But I didn't have time to worry about that now. I had work to do!

Living with my parents, I had learned how to investigate a crime scene. I knew the first thing was to secure the area.

Raising my voice again, I told the crowd, "I want everyone to leave the scene at once, except for you

four." I pointed to Charles, the man with the fur coat, Mr. Kartier, and the feathered woman. These four people stepped forward. The feathered woman was smiling as if she'd just been named Miss Hunter Island. The other guests, including Asyla, wandered back to the mansion.

I placed each of the four people I had selected at different corners of the scene, creating a large box around the area.

"What are we doing?" Mr. Kartier asked from his corner.

"Don't let anyone by you until I say it's all right," I answered. "Do you understand?"

They all nodded. The scene was now secure.

Next on my list of things to do at a crime scene: Gather evidence.

I soon discovered the plane itself held no clues. It was, as I'd first observed, completely empty. There were no bags. No food supplies for a long trip over the Atlantic. No signs of life whatsoever.

Nothing.

I expanded my search for clues to the area outside the plane. The squishy ground around the craft had been trampled by all the guests. But I could still make out the tracks left by the plane.

June 13, 1925

Realizing I was running out of time, I hunkered down for a closer look at these tracks. The storm clouds were swirling overhead as if preparing for the next downpour. Another heavy rain could wash away even these deep tracks.

I took out my notebook and made this quick sketch.

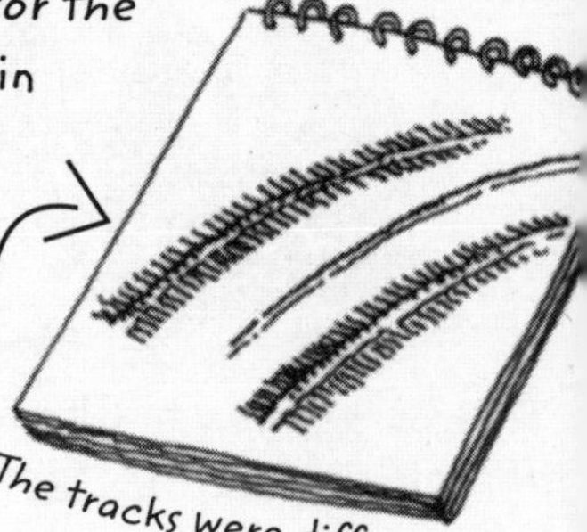

The tracks were different.

Examining the tracks more closely, I saw they didn't match up with the landing I had sketched earlier. The tracks I was looking at ran from the wheels of the plane off to the side of the airstrip where they disappeared.

But how could that be? From inside the Great Hall, a group of people, including me, had watched the plane land. We had all seen the craft touch down at the back of the airstrip—not at the side—and roll to a stop.

Maybe I had sketched the landing wrong.

And how could a crime be committed in secret right under the noses of so many witnesses?

That's it! I realized. The answer could be with one of the other hundred witnesses. They might have seen something without knowing it was the key to solving the case.

Just then the rain started to come down again. Deciding I had gathered all the evidence I could, I called to the four people standing guard, "Thank you for your time! We can all go back inside now."

The five of us rushed back to the mansion as the sky opened up. Inside the Great Hall, I stopped a tired-looking maid who was carrying a tray of dirty glasses.

"Have you seen Miss Pinkteron?" I asked her.

"She's upstairs with Mr. Hatherford," the maid said, stifling a yawn. "Poor man says he's having chest pains."

"Has anyone called for medical help?"

She shook her head. "The phone lines are down. And no help could reach us anyway until the waters calm."

"One of the guests must be a doctor," I said, thinking of all the swanky people at the party.

"Sure," the sleepy-eyed maid told me. "But he's a dermatologist. Miss Pinkerton said she'd stay with Mr. Hatherford until she can get him to relax."

I thanked her, and the maid wandered off.

It looked like I would have to continue my solo investigation. And that meant interviewing the guests—

TEC TIP

GET RESULTS!

- Interviewing suspects and looking to crack the case FAST? Then just follow LASTS:
- Listen! Be an active listener. Really hear what people say and how they say it.
- Ask! Your questions should always have a point, but shouldn't be too leading.
- Shut up! Do not interrupt. Let the subject talk and talk—this can be the best way to learn information.
- Train your eyes! Maintain eye contact. It's harder for someone to lie effectively when you're looking directly at him or her.
- Stay awake! Be attentive. You don't want to miss a single twitch or word the subject says.

who were not only witnesses to a possible crime but also potential suspects!

I created a comfortable space in one corner of the Great Hall. I placed two overstuffed chairs so that they faced each other next to a fireplace. Then, one by one, I started interviewing guests and staff members.

I invited each person to sit and offered him or her a glass of water. Many people, like Mrs. Kartier, didn't seem to grasp the seriousness of the situation. She just kept giggling, as if it were a game. Other people, like the man in the fur coat, seemed so eager to play detective that I felt certain they were making up or at least

MY INTERVIEW WITH MR. VIRGIL GATES, 1:40 AM:

G. CODD FITZMORGAN: Why are you here?

VIRGIL GATES: (nervous laugh) You asked me to be.

GCF: No, Mr. Gates, not in that chair. I mean, Why are you here at this party?

VG: I don't have to answer your questions.

GCF: Are you hiding something?

VG: Of course not. (pause) Fine. I'm an old friend of John's.

GCF: Really?

VG: (looking away) Well, maybe not a "friend," but we do business together. In fact, I've hired John and Justine's delivery company to do some work for me.

GCF: And Asyla Notabe? Does she have any ideas about what happened to John?

VG: Who knows what that woman thinks.

GCF: Isn't she your girlfriend?

VG: Yes. But if you think that means I understand her, you've got another think coming.

June 13, 1925

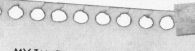

MY INTERVIEW WITH MANG ZE MAGNIFICO, 1:55 A.M.:

GCF: What is your real name?

MANG ZE MAGNIFICO: Monsieur Mang ze Magnifico.

GCF: That's the name that appears on your birth certificate?

MZM: You are more zan velcome to fly to France and check.

GCF: Did you see anything odd?

MZM: I always zee ze odd somethings.

GCF: I mean especially odd about John Hatherford's airplane landing.

MZM: Jean-Claude, he iz unhappy. Ze spirit wants hiz answers, and he vaz interrupted by a little boy.

GCF: What technique do you use to speak with the spirits? Table turning or desk gyrations?

MZM: Ze desk gyrations.

GCF: Now that is odd.

MZM: Why, little boy, iz that?

GCF: Because I just made desk gyrations up. It doesn't exist.

MZM: (stands up and leaves the interview area)

exaggerating what they had seen. Still others, such as Charles, provided excellent objective observations that helped me re-create events in my mind.

Here are two of the interviews I recorded in my spiral notebook.

Who should I interview next? I wondered, looking around the Great Hall. I spotted Asyla Notabe, munching

on spoonfuls of caviar at a food table.

It was clear she had something against me and might be tough to interview. But I again reminded myself that a good detective has to deal with the good and the bad. So I made my way over to her.

Asyla loves cavi

"Miss Notabe," I said politely, "can I can ask you a few questions?"

She smiled at me with her bright red lips and popped a mound of caviar in her mouth. Her perfectly shaped eyes squinted in delight. She chewed, swallowed, and finally answered my question. "No."

Once again I was confused by her. "What?" I asked.

"Honey, you don't have the authority to make me do a thing." She picked a piece of lint off the shoulder of my tuxedo. "I'll tell you what. You can ask me one or two questions if you let me interview you first."

I noticed she never made direct eye contact. "Why?"

"I'm bored." She shrugged.

Bored? A roaring party in a mansion, a violent storm, a dramatic landing after a historic flight, and the disappearance of the pilot—and she was bored?

"What would you want to know about me?" I asked her. "You don't seem to like me much."

Her lower lip jutted out slightly. "Why would you go and say that, silly boy?"

Because it's true, I thought. But I said aloud, "The séance, the landing strip, the way you've been speaking to me."

"Oh, that. To be honest, I'm a little out of sorts here.

Your dear friend Justine Pinkerton and I go way back. Did you know she was on that same train where I met your parents? I wasn't sure how she'd react to me showing up at her fancy party."

"I'm sure that Judge is glad you're here."

"Is that so?" Asyla's face still had the sweet smile, but I wondered if it was honey for a trap. Then again, what choice did I have? She might have witnessed something important to the investigation.

"Okay, you can ask me questions first," I agreed. "Let's go over to the chairs I've set up."

Asyla said, "I'd rather stay here, next to the caviar."

Other people in the room were now looking at us curiously. With all these celebrities around, glamorous Asyla was choosing to chitchat with me. It was exciting!

"Let's start," she said. "I adore the way you put that awful Mang in his place. How does a child know so much about Houdini?"

I hesitated before answering her. "I used to have claustrophobia. It started when I was six. Small rooms, snug blankets, tiny automobiles—stuff like that could send me into fits of panic. I felt like I couldn't get out. Then my mom showed me that I was smart enough to 'detect' my way out of any situation."

"Ah, your mom." Asyla's face remained frozen in a masklike smile. "Please go on."

"She told me I didn't need to

I can get out of anyplace!

panic. I have sleuthing skills in my blood. I'd never find myself in a jam I couldn't get out of. So I started training to be an escape artist. My mom would stay close by, and I'd lock myself in rooms and attempt to 'escape.' After a few years, it got awfully hard to find any locked room that could hold me."

Asyla clapped her hands together. "I get it. So Harry Houdini, the master escape artist, is your hero! Your mother is very clever. Is that why you use her name as your last name?"

"The name on my birth certificate is Godfrey Codd Moorie," I said.

Asyla let out a giggle that sounded like a wind chime and then covered her mouth. "Oh. Did I just laugh out loud? So sorry."

Shrugging, I said, "I got used to other kids making fun of my name. When I turned twelve, my parents told me I could choose my own name." I spoke quickly now, eager to get to the part where I got to interview her. "I decided if I was going to be a detective I should have a name that sounds mysterious. I shortened Godfrey to G. For my last name, I put together my mom's first name, Fitz, and her maiden name, Morgan, into my new last name, Fitzmorgan."

"Your father must have been hurt that you didn't choose his name." She giggled again, but this time the sound had a few false notes.

~~Fitz G. Morgan~~

~~G. Codd~~

~~G Mooriegan~~

~~Morgan Fitz~~

✓ G. Codd Fitzmorgan

June 13, 1925

I was starting to feel pretty uncomfortable. "Actually, Dad congratulated me on my choice. Now, I just have a few questions," I said before she could ask me anything else.

Asyla beamed at me. "Two."

"What?"

"I said I would answer one or two questions, not a few," she told me. "Since I'm feeling kind, I'll answer two. Let's test your detective skills. Make the questions good ones."

Only two questions allowed.

For the first time during our conversation, her eyes met mine. I could see something prowling around behind her gaze.

She made me feel scattered, and I blurted, "Did you notice anything strange tonight?"

Asyla held up one finger and mumbled something through a mouthful of fish eggs.

"What?" I couldn't understand her.

She triumphantly held up two fingers as she swallowed. "We're all done. I answered your first question, 'Did you notice anything strange?' with a 'No.' And I'll answer your second question, 'What?' with, 'I said no.'"

This was unbelievable! Before I could protest, Asyla had turned her back on me. "Thanks for the fun chat," she said over her shoulder. "Beat it."

And that was that. The interview was over, and I was left with no answers—just one more question. Was Asyla involved in John's disappearance?

Someone was skulking around outside!

June 13, 1925

2:30 AM

Before questioning the next witness, I moved the chairs a little away from the fire. It was very late, and the warmth of the flames was making me drowsy. I needed to stay alert!

For my eleventh interview, I asked a parlor maid to take a seat. She was still holding a few of the boxes she was moving up to Judge's room.

"These are engagement presents." The maid gestured toward the boxes. "I just wonder if there'll be a wedding now that the groom has been kidnapped!"

I needed to keep rumors to a minimum. "Right now, this is a missing persons case. We are not sure that anyone has been nabbed. There is no ransom note. There is no sign of a struggle. It is as if John Hatherford simply vanished into—" I stopped midsentence. Through the open double doors, I could see that someone was wandering around the crime scene.

I jumped up and ran to the doors. "You!" I shouted. Whoever it was could be disturbing valuable evidence. "Get away from that plane!"

The person turned. I could see that it was a man. He seemed startled by my call, and he began running away from the crime scene and toward the woods in back of the house.

In my opinion, the only people who run away have something to hide.

I think I am fairly courageous but no fool. This man was easily three times my size. Charles and the chauffeur were waiting to be interviewed.

"We have to stop that man! He might be a suspect!" I called to them. The three of us headed out the door. Moments later, Charles and the chauffeur each had one of the man's arms and were escorting him into the Great Hall. The man had dark curly hair and a mischievous look on his face. It was as if he knew a wonderful secret and was just bursting to share it.

I thought, now we're getting somewhere! A suspect.

I asked him to take a seat in the chair opposite me, and I began the interview.

"Who are you?" I asked.

"John Baird." It was clear at once from his thick accent that he was Scottish.

"What were you doing by that airplane?"

"Is it not the one? Ence mare I am lest," the man said.

I had no idea what he meant. "I'm sorry," I said. "But what did you say?"

"Ence mare I am lest, are ye def, laddy?" The man's Scottish accent was so thick, it was difficult for me to

Mang

make heads or tails of what he was saying. He continued, "Ded ye and the other kiddies enjoy the poppet shew?"

Before I could ask about this odd question, I was interrupted by Mang, who was standing within earshot. "Listen to ze funny vay he iz talking!"

"Please, Mr. Mang, let me complete my interview!" I snapped. I thought I might be getting somewhere with this Scotsman.

Suddenly, lightning flashed and reflected off the Scotsman's crystal lapel pin—and there was a sparkly flash of blue light! The Scotsman must be the figure I saw appear and vanish in the parlor!

Now I would get some answers!

And then the lights went out. The Great Hall was plunged into total darkness.

People screamed in terror. Near me there was a loud scuffling sound and a muffled cry as if someone was shouting through a piece of cloth—

"Who is there?" I shouted, but doubted my voice could be heard over the guests as they panicked and tried to find their way out the room.

Just as I thought the screaming was becoming unbearable, the room exploded with light.

Men and women around me stopped yelling. I gaped at the empty seat in front of me.

June 13, 1925

The Scotsman was gone.

"Where is he?" I asked the man in the fur coat, who had crawled under a table. He shrugged.

From the sounds I had heard when the lights were out, I was betting someone had nabbed the Scotsman. And just as I was getting close to some answers!

"What is it?" Judge called from the top of the grand staircase. Spotting me, she rushed down the steps. "What is it, G. Codd? Why were so many people shouting? Have you found John?"

I quickly told her about the recent events. I started with the Scotsman's appearance by the plane and finished with his mysterious vanishing.

Judge shook her head in confusion. "A Scotsman? Do you think this man is somehow connected with John's disappearance?"

I shrugged. "Honestly, I don't know what to think. It's what I feel."

A small smile touched Judge's lips. "Now you sound like your father. A detective's heart is one of his most powerful assets."

My father
A detective's heart is one of his most powerful assets.

"How are you holding up, Judge?"

Judge put a cooling hand to her forehead. "I finally calmed Mr. Hatherford. A nurse is with him, watching over him while he sleeps. But I. . . I need to do something, G. Codd. Otherwise, I'm going to go crazy with worry." She took a deep breath. "I need to find out what happened to John."

If a plan of action would help Judge get through this, then I was her man. "I think our first step is to find the Scotsman. He was involved in the most recent disappearance. The clues will still be fresh."

I asked Charles to join us. Together, we organized a few of the guests remaining in the Great Hall into a search party. Twenty of us fanned out across the room, knocking on the floor, looking for hidden trapdoors, and pounding on walls, searching for signs of secret doors. We scoured the Great Hall looking for any sign of what had happened to the Scotsman.

But there was nothing.

The searchers grew bored with a game that offered no immediate reward. They began to scatter. Judge and I met near one of the fireplaces.

INVESTIGATION ACADEMY 101

SEARCH PARTY

Line up your searchers so that they are shoulder to shoulder. Tell them not to be afraid to rub up against each other. The closer they are, the less they will miss.

This formation is effective outside and in large spaces. If done correctly, not an inch of ground will be skipped.

June 13, 1925

Virgil gazing at Asyla

"I'm going to check on Mr. Hatherford. I'll be right back," Judge said. She was leaving the room when I heard Asyla's sarcastic voice.

"This is a great party, really swanky!" she was telling Virgil, who gazed at her with dreamy fascination.

They were lounging on one of the fur-covered couches in front of the dying fire. Asyla was picking up party favors, like hats and noisemakers, and throwing them onto the flames. Lazily, she crumpled up a streamer and tossed it toward the fire. The paper bounced off the high back wall of the fireplace and rolled by my feet.

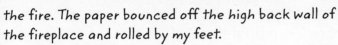

"What are you doing?" I asked Asyla.

She ignored me and turning to her boyfriend, said, "Make him go away, Virgil."

Obediently, Virgil made a small gesture that I should shoo. But I didn't need him to tell me. I had had enough of Asyla's games and left on my own.

Deciding to update my journal, I took a seat on a nearby sofa.

Now, as I try to stop yawning, a plan of action is taking shape in my head. It might put me in more danger than I've ever encountered.

It's important that I stay awake to work on the plan.

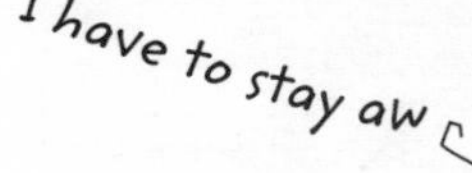

Asleep in the Great Hall

June 13, 1925

9:05 AM

I must have fallen asleep!

I jerked awake. It took me a second or two to remember where I was and what was happening.

How could I have slept? I guess the events of yesterday must have been too much for me. The scare on the ferry, the séance, the party—John's disappearance!

Instantly, I felt a sharp pang of guilt. I had let Judge down. I had fallen asleep when I should have been cracking the case.

Outside, it was so dark it could have been early evening. But according to my pocket watch (a gift from Dad), it was morning. Rain pelted the room's only window, and I could see tree branches swaying back and forth in the violent gusts of wind. The chimneys of the now-cold fireplaces moaned as the wind blew through them, like instruments in a creepy orchestra.

The Great Hall was nearly deserted. One or two other guests had fallen asleep on couches, and a large man snored loudly in the far corner. The rest of the guests must be in their rooms.

Someone, probably Judge, had covered me with a blanket.

I was just getting up to find Judge when she entered the Great Hall. Wearing a simple gray dress with a purple scarf, she came quickly down the stairs to join me. She carried herself with perfect posture, as always. But there were dark circles under her eyes.

"Judge!" I stood up as she approached and gave me a peck on the cheek. "Good morning, G. Codd," she said. Reading the look on my face, she added, "Don't be upset that I didn't wake you earlier. I need your mind fresh and rested. We still have to find John."

"So, there's been no sign of him?"

"No, nothing," Judge said sadly.

So it must be foul play, I thought. Even the most skeptical person would have to admit now that this wasn't a joke of some kind. John was definitely missing—or kidnapped.

Gesturing toward the small window, Judge said, "And the storm's grown even worse. There's still no way to get back to the mainland, or for the police to get out here."

"Well, that's good in one way, isn't it? If John has been nabbed, the kidnappers can't get him off the island."

She nodded. "Here, I brought you these from the kitchen." She handed me a small basketful of bread puffs that oozed a jam filling. "Strawberry jam used to be your mom's favorite."

We sat down on the couch and I bit into a puff. Delicious! Just what I needed to get my mind moving. "How is Mr. Hatherford?" I asked.

Yum!!

"He's doing better," she said. "He actually managed to eep for an hour or two. And I've convinced him he on't do John any good by getting up and having a eart attack."

"How about you, Judge? How are you dealing with verything?"

She took a breath before answering. "It just doesn't eem real to me. My fiancé has vanished. There are still ighty guests here, but we've cancelled all the festivities. /eren't we supposed to be having the time of our lives his weekend?"

I didn't know what to say. We were quiet for a ioment. The only sounds were the falling rain and the iores of the sleeping guest in the corner.

I decided to turn to a topic where I could be seful—the investigation. "Judge, can you think of nyone who would want to kidnap John?"

Judge looked relieved to sink her teeth into etective work. "I've been trying to come up with a list ll night. You met John last summer when we visited your ottage in Michigan. You know what he's like. Everyone ants to be his friend. No one would want to hurt him."

I nodded. It was true. John had a way of charming nyone. But maybe his disappearance had nothing to do ith his personality. "He has all that money," I said.

"The money is mostly his father's," Judge said. "And if e were kidnapped for money, why hasn't there been a ansom note?"

I tried a new approach. "So you can't think of anyone e's been fighting with?"

"Well, yes." Judge said. "I can think of one person."

"Who?" I asked eagerly.

"Me," answered Judge, giving me a little smile when she saw the surprise on my face. "It's okay, G. Codd. I love John and how brave he is. But I've been upset about the chances he takes in that airplane of his. Then there's the fact that he doesn't want me to go to law school."

"Why wouldn't John want you to be a lawyer?" I asked.

Something flashed in Judge's green eyes. "Office work is okay in his mind. But John doesn't think law is for women. Of course, I don't let anyone make decisions like that for me. In the end it was my choice. I decided not to go so I could spend more time with him—at the office and after work."

She shook her head as if to clear her thoughts. "We need a break in this case. Let's look at the clues we have."

Starting with the airplane, we talked about the evidence we had gathered so far. We both agreed the plane seemed to be a dead end. Judge had gone back out there this morning and searched for clues.

"Not that I don't trust your work, G. Codd," she assured me. "I just had to see the empty plane for myself."

"Unfortunately," I said, "my interviews don't seem to have gotten us anywhere, either." I handed her my notebook with the witness interviews.

She flipped through them, reading each one carefully. "You did some terrific detective work here, G. Codd." She stopped on one page. "You spoke to Asyla?"

I caught something in her tone. "Do you think Asyla had something to do with John's disappearance?"

She shook her head. "No, but remember, the most

beautiful creatures in nature can sometimes have the strongest venom."

That sounded alarming. "What do you mean?"

"Not to worry," Judge said. "We should keep an eye on her, that's all."

She stood up and began pacing. "About the only thing we can conclude with certainty is that yesterday was full of mysteries. If there were just one of them that we could explain..."

Did Judge suspect Asyla?

I thought of the plan I had been working on in my head. "There just might be one. I think the Scotsman is the figure I saw vanish during the séance. You and I both examined the corner where he disappeared, remember? There are no doors or windows, so he must have used a secret passage to get out. If we find the passage, it could lead us to the Scotsman, and he might be able to answer our questions."

After a moment's thought, Judge said, "Sounds good, G. Codd. Let's go check it out."

Quickly, we climbed the stairs of the Great Hall. We made our way to the parlor where the séance had been held. We gave the corner of the room another long look, but after ten minutes, we still couldn't find any sign of a secret passage.

It was time to put the plan that I had been working on into action.

I looked at Judge, hoping she would continue to trust in me. "I think I have a—"

"You have a plan," she interrupted. "But, you're about to say that your plan is kind of unconventional. Am I right?"

"How did you know?" I asked.

She gave me a grin. "The apple doesn't fall far from the tree. What do you need?"

I reminded her about the training Mom had given me, helping me learn to escape from impossible situations.

"I want you to close me in here and lock the door," I told Judge. "That will put me in the right state of mind and force my strongest sleuthing skills into action. If there's a way out of this room, I'll find it."

She thought it over, and then she said, "All right, but I'm going to add a safety net."

Judge went to a shelf and picked up what looked like two vials stacked on top of each other. "See this timer? When I turn it over, the sand will take exactly ten minutes to run from the top to the bottom. That's how long you have to be alone in here. Then I'm coming in—"

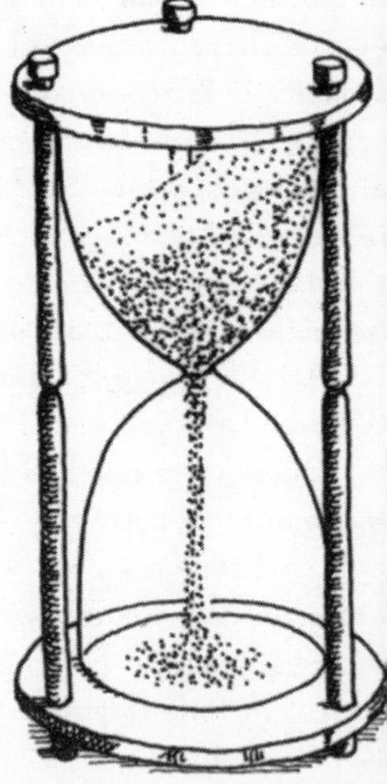

"But I need to feel like I'm trapped." I protested.

She wouldn't budge. "Then use your imagination, G. Codd. There could be a kidnapper roaming about the mansion's secret passages, and people are disappearing. I don't want you alone in this room for too long. You've got ten minutes."

I nodded. "All right," I said. "I'm ready to do this."

Looking at her watch, Judge turned the timer over and placed it on a table where I could see it. She gave me a quick pat on the shoulder. Then she left the room and closed the door behind her.

With a CLUNK! the lock slid into place.

Why did the radio have three dials?

June 13, 1925

12:35 PM

My eyes slid over to the corner of the parlor where the Scotsman had first disappeared. I examined the bookshelf, the radio, the thick rug, the tapestry...

But I kept coming back to the same thing. The timer.

This wasn't working. This was a stupid idea. I couldn't concentrate. I kept worrying about how much time I had left.

Who can tell time on a sand timer anyway?

Focus! I told myself. *You've done this type of thing many times before!*

I calmed myself down. With steadier vision I took a new look at the corner.

A large bookshelf stood against one wall. In many detective stories, the hero simply has to pull on one of the books, and a secret door pops open. It was worth a try. But not surprisingly, nothing happened.

A radio sat against the other wall. I'd seen plenty of these—after all there were about five million of them in the United States. People everywhere turned them on when they wanted news or entertainment. This model looked old-fashioned and had probably belonged to the rumrunner. I tapped the radio and was rewarded with a hollow sound.

I looked closely at its dials. There were three dials to tune in the correct frequency. What kind of radio used

three dials that each did exactly the same thing? That would be like having three steering wheels in your automobile.

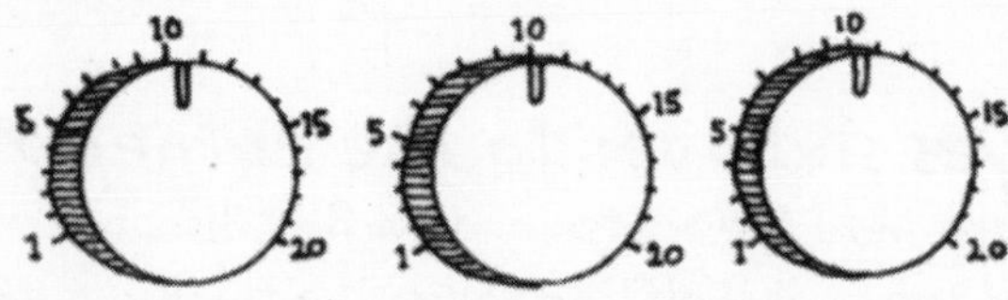

Numbers on each of the dials ran from 1 to 20. I gave one of the dials a twist. I heard the soft clicking of tumblers. The dials had to be part of some kind of combination lock that required the correct sequence of three numbers to open. What it was guarding, I didn't know. I just knew I wanted to crack it open.

What three numbers would be important to a rumrunner?

I had to think fast. If I ran out of time and Judge came into the room, I might snap out of this focused mental state. Then we'd be back at square one.

People often used three numbers to indicate a specific date. The Great War ended on 11/11/18, which stood for November 11, 1918.

But what about a rumrunner? What date would he use? His birthday? If that were the case, I realized I'd be in trouble. How could I ever guess that?

And then it hit me.

I started spinning the dials, getting them to read

1 16 20

This was probably one of the most important dates to a rumrunner—January 16, 1920. The date Prohibition went into effect.

June 13, 1925

I turned the last dial to read 20—

Hot socks!

A narrow rectangle in the wall to the right of the radio popped open. It had been perfectly disguised, by the carved design of the wall. Without thinking about it, I turned my body to the side, so I could fit, and stepped through the doorway.

It was dark in there after the parlor, and I stretched out my hands in front of me. They found nothing. Only the empty air of a secret passage that stretched ahead of me. But to either side, my fingers touched cold, slightly damp brick.

Glancing back into the parlor I could see the last grains of sand running down the timer. I took another step into the passage. My right thumb ran along a brick that gave slightly. I put more pressure on the brick. With a small of whoosh of air and a click—

The door swung shut behind me.

Suddenly the thing I had been trying so hard to imagine in the parlor was real. Far too real. I was now trapped in a dark, narrow, frightening place.

My heart gave a few lurches like a bootlegger's getaway car kicking into overdrive. I felt like someone had tied thick ropes around my chest and was slowly tightening them. The panic was familiar—this was the start of a claustrophobia attack, like the ones I had suffered as a kid.

I called on all my years of training with my mom to stop the attack before it started. Her words played in my head, a soothing song to calm my heart.

You are a detective. And a detective solves problems.

problems that other people think are impossible. You can find your way out of anything!

Within moments, I regained control. My heart stopped battering my ribs. Ah...that's better, I thought. I took a look at my surroundings.

At least I tried to. With the light from the parlor gone, it was too dark in the small area to find the inside latch of the hidden door. I could only see a dim glow from up ahead. About 30 feet in front of me, a stone spiral staircase slithered its way up an interior tower.

I could wait for Judge to open the door to the parlor and pound on the secret door until she discovered me.

Or I could investigate. John could be tied up somewhere in here. He might need my help this second. Proving that I had really beaten my fears, I walked slowly away from the hidden door and toward the stairs.

I started up the steps, moving very slowly. Any one of them might be a trap, giving way when my foot stepped on it, and I would fall and fall...

Then I reached the top of a tower. Now I could see where the gloomy light was coming from. Two large windows had been built into opposite sides of the tower. The tower, hidden among the chimneys and turrets on the roof, must have been used by the rumrunner to hide—or as a lookout for approaching authorities.

But the windows had now been covered with thick black curtains. One of these had shifted and let in some of the gray afternoon light. I pulled a curtain back to peer outside. The stormy winds continued, but the rain had stopped.

I stepped further into the room, and a string brushed

against my face. I gave it a pull. It was connected to an electric bulb, and the room filled with light.

My eyes took a moment to adjust to the brightness. Cables and lighting devices snaked here and there along the heavy stone walls of the tiny room. Surprised by the modern equipment, I turned and found myself staring directly at something even stranger.

A flat piece of wood about five feet by five feet lay on top of two sawhorses. The surface of the wood was covered with miniature trees, fake grass, a tiny airstrip...

And a little toy plane attached to thin wires.

It looked like this:

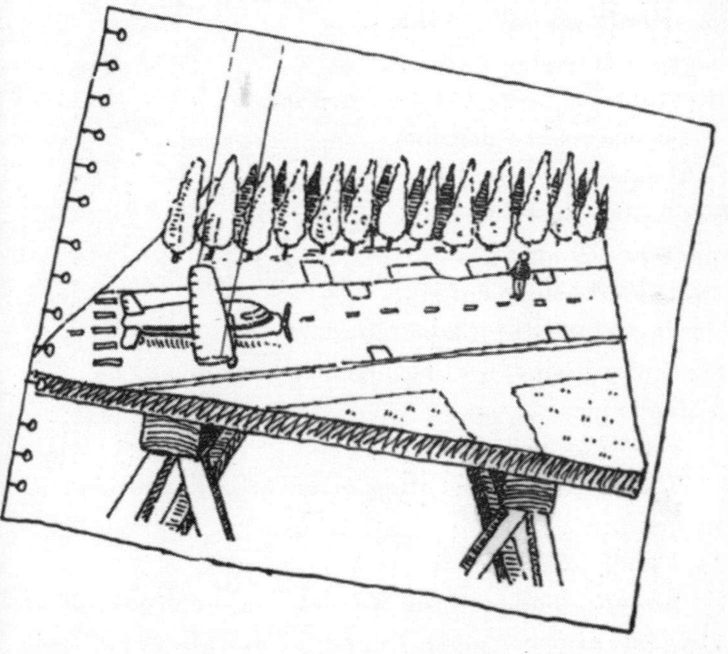

It was a model of the property right outside the Great Hall.

I took a step closer and touched the puppet of a pilot. About the size of a frankfurter, this mini flyboy was dressed just like John.

"Ded ye enjoy the poppet shew?" The Scotsman's words rang out in my head. Had he meant "puppet" when he said "poppet"?

This must be some kind of puppet stage. But who would be able to see it at the top of this secluded, secret tower?

Nothing makes sense, I thought. I looked around the room for answers. Almost immediately, I noticed the huge camera pointed at the stage.

DETECTIVE NEWS FLASH

SOMETHING'S IN THE AIR!

This year marked the first succe television broadcast! In a London Scotsman John Logie Baird sen image of a puppet from one roon another. Just imagine what this can m for detectives and security guards w want to keep an eye on a distant locatic

Dad would be drooling right now, I thought. He was really into modern machinery. In fact, I'd read about equipment like this in one of his books. Dad would see this as a window of opportunity to examine technology—

Wait a second!

The words "window of opportunity" rolled around in my head.

Then I got it!

Someone had used the "window" in the Great Hall as a window of opportunity. This person must have put some kind of receiver in the window frame. When we had watched the plane landing through the small window in the Great Hall, we hadn't actually seen outside. We had been looking into something called a "television screen."

I thought back to JENNY, John's plane out on the airstrip. That airplane was real. I had reached out and touched it. The plane existed. That was a fact.

But the landing of that real plane had been faked!

I was convinced that someone had used this puppet stage and the camera to make us think we had seen John's plane land.

Why? I had no idea. But I couldn't wait to share this discovery with Judge.

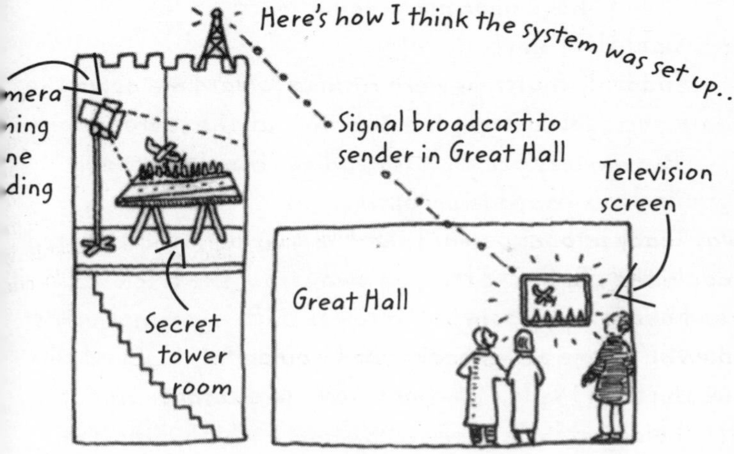

I headed toward the stairs. Not wanting to alert anyone that I'd been in the tower, I pulled on the string. Without the electric light, the room was thrown back into darkness. The only illumination came from the small crack in the curtains.

June 13, 1925

Sliding my hand firmly along the wall to steady myself, I began my descent down the spiral staircase. Now that I knew where I was going, my feet moved more confidently. I reached the bottom quickly.

I took a few steps toward the secret door—

Screep!

It was the sound of the hard sole of a shoe scraping on the rough floor.

Someone else was in the passage with me.

"Judge...?" I whispered. But the darkness seemed to absorb my voice like a sponge.

For what seemed like forever, I stood still and listened. Nothing.

It must have been my imagination—

Slap! Slap! Slap!

Suddenly footsteps were rushing toward me down the dark passageway from the direction of the secret door.

The mystery person was heading straight for me!

Panic exploded in my brain.

I looked back toward the dim gray light that filtered down the stairs, and stepped away from the brick wall. Just then the curtain in the tower shifted—either on its own or by someone's hand—and completely blocked the window. All the light in the passageway disappeared.

I was instantly disoriented, unsure which direction I faced.

Footsteps echoed all around me. Someone was coming straight at me, and I wasn't even sure from which way!

In the pitch dark, I reached out for the wall. I made contact and pressed my body flat against the hard brick. I hoped my pursuer would pass by without noticing me.

June 13, 1925

To my complete surprise, the wall didn't resist. Instead, it gave way, and then I was falling through it. Had I just broken through the wall? A gentle click let me know this was not the case. Leading from the passageway to the outside, a door-shaped section of the brick had swung gently open.

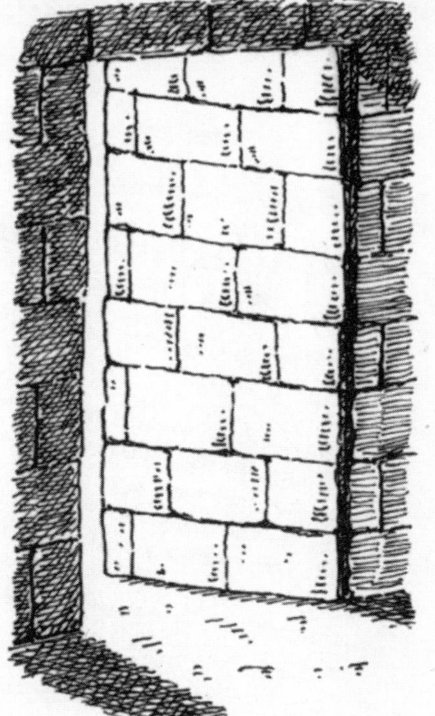

Another secret door!

Luckily, I had discovered another secret door, this one completely by accident.

The wet ground sucked hungrily at my shoes as the brick door behind me swung closed again. The shape of the door disappeared into the wall, making it nearly impossible to discover.

A scratching sound brought my attention back to the wall. I listened closely.

Someone was clawing at the secret door, trying to get it to open.

What should I do?

I decided I was better off standing my ground.

June 13, 1925

Turning to the door, I adopted a defensive stance my father had taught me.

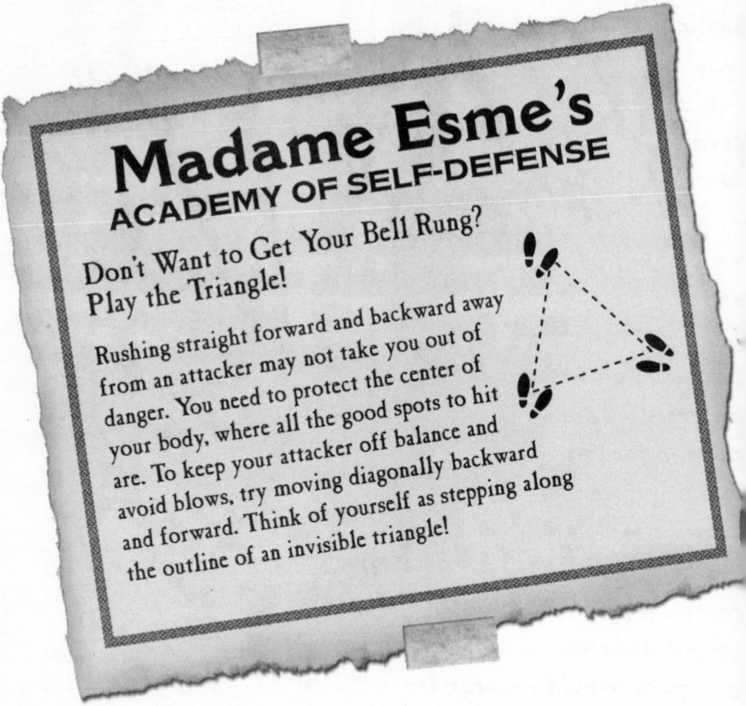

Madame Esme's
ACADEMY OF SELF-DEFENSE

Don't Want to Get Your Bell Rung? Play the Triangle!

Rushing straight forward and backward away from an attacker may not take you out of danger. You need to protect the center of your body, where all the good spots to hit are. To keep your attacker off balance and avoid blows, try moving diagonally backward and forward. Think of yourself as stepping along the outline of an invisible triangle!

Click! I heard the secret door's lock unlatch—

The door was swinging open—I held my breath and braced myself for the worst—

"G. Codd!"

Out of the darkness, a face framed by blond hair came into view. It was Judge! The door closed behind her. She rushed to me and took my hand. "You scared me to death. What would I tell your parents if you'd gone missing, too?"

June 13, 1925

I couldn't stop grinning in relief. "Judge, you're the cat's pajamas! I was sure I was being followed by the villain."

Judge leaned in close, her voice turning deadly serious as she said, "You were, G. Codd. And so was I."

"What?" I managed to ask.

"I heard footsteps chasing me through the passage," she whispered. "There is a third person in there, right on my heels."

We both turned to the secret door and waited for Judge's mysterious pursuer to join us.

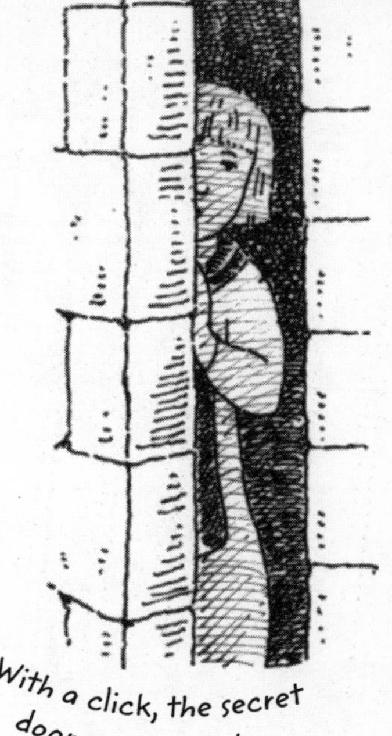

With a click, the secret door swung open!

Long, terrifying seconds passed as Judge and I kept our positions.

Who would emerge from the secret passage? Would we be able to subdue him or her? Would the person have a weapon and attack us?

The wind whistled, clouds blew overhead, distant waves crashed against the island's shore. But no one opened the hidden door.

"Whoever it was must have turned back," Judge said.

I didn't know whether to be disappointed or relieved. We had no way of opening the door from this side, so we turned our thoughts to the investigation.

The hidden airstrip!

June 13, 1925

2:10 PM

"G. Codd, what did you discover?" Judge asked.

I described the items I had found in the tower's broadcast room. I told her I thought they'd been used to trick the guests into thinking they were watching the plane land.

"You mean John might not even have landed at all? He could be lost at sea or..." Her voice trailed off.

Not knowing what to say, I glanced around. We were somewhere behind the mansion. Tall, dark pine trees loomed over us, their branches whipping in the wind. Suddenly we heard a strange flapping noise coming from the forest.

"What's that?" Judge asked.

"I don't know," I said, "but I think we'd better go and find out." Cautiously we made our way through the dim light under the trees.

"Look—up ahead—I think there's a clearing," Judge said softly.

We broke through the trees and found ourselves standing on the edge a long, grassy field. I took in the wind socks flapping in the wind, and the trees that had been cleared to create a long, rectangular space.

"It's a hidden airstrip!" I said. The questions in my mind quadrupled as I looked down toward the end of the runway. I could barely see the outline of a large object sitting there.

Judge and I went to take a look. A tarp made of camouflage material covered a giant lump underneath. By now it was pretty clear what the lump was.

Together, we pulled at the wet tarp—and found ourselves face to propeller with an aircraft.

"Another plane!" I cried. I noticed it was the same model as JENNY, John's airplane. "Did you know about this?"

"No," Judge answered. "I've been here many times and I never even knew there was another airstrip. From the looks of those stumps, the trees were just recently cut down to create this landing area."

"Let's look inside," I said. The door opened easily, and I peered into the cockpit. The fuel gauge read full. But the inside of this airplane was as empty as the other one. At least that's what I thought until I noticed an object that must have rolled to the back of the storage area.

I lifted the bottle carefully by its lip, not wanting to disturb any existing fingerprints.

"Can I have your handkerchief, G. Codd?"

I fished it out of my pocket with my other hand and

gave it to her. She wrapped her right hand in the cloth and carefully took the bottle from me, not wanting to smudge or destroy any evidence.

Judge held the bottle under her nose and winced. "It's Scotch," she said.

"What?" I had heard her, but I found it hard to believe.

She nodded. "There was a kind of whiskey in this bottle. You can still smell it. If the bottle wasn't empty, it'd be illegal to even be holding it. It would also be extremely valuable on the black market."

"But it is empty..."

"Thank goodness. For a moment, I thought John might be mixed up in something," Judge said. "But this isn't even his plane! His plane is outside the Great Hall, so where did this one come from?"

"Is it from the fleet of your air courier business?" I asked. "Maybe it's here to make a delivery?"

Her eyes narrowed as she scrutinized the craft. "I don't recognize it. But I brought the business records and books with me this weekend. I had planned to go over a few things with John's father. The books are in my room. Let's go check and see whether this type of plane is listed there."

With Judge carrying the bottle, the two of us started back toward the house. Just then a thought struck me, and I stopped.

"What is it?" Judge asked.

"Wait one second," I told her, turning back to the second airplane. "I have to grab something."

Back in the Great Hall

June 13, 1925

7:20 PM

The Great Hall was quiet. Several butlers scurried about the room, but there were no guests in sight. They must still have been in their rooms.

Or vanished, I thought to myself.

Judge and I made our way up the grand staircase to the main part of the mansion. She insisted that we stop in the kitchen for something to eat.

Minutes later, after we had wolfed down roast beef sandwiches, we were moving again. To get to Judge's room we had to make our way through a twisting maze of hallways and staircases.

By the time we reached her room, we were both beat. "It will just take a second," Judge was saying as she pushed open the door. She froze. My mouth dropped open at what I saw inside.

As she had asked, the staff had brought the engagement presents up to Judge's room. At that time, they were all still wrapped. That was no longer the case.

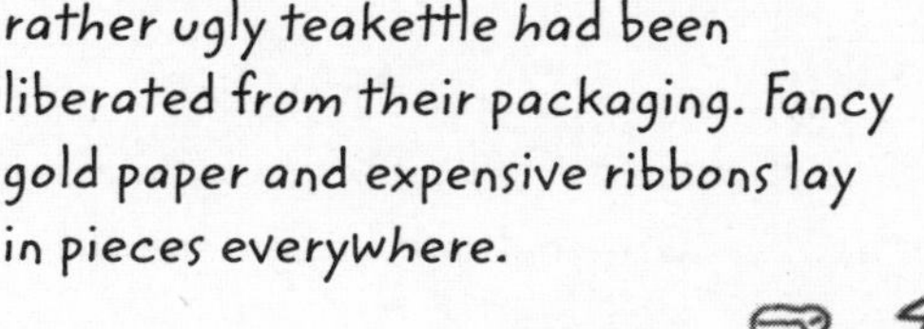

Among other things, a silver goblet and a rather ugly teakettle had been liberated from their packaging. Fancy gold paper and expensive ribbons lay in pieces everywhere.

Asyla was opening Judge's presents!

And who was the cause of all this chaos?

None other than Asyla Notabe. Perched on Judge's bed, Asyla was busy trying to open one of the boxes she had just unwrapped. It was the large box I'd seen in the back parlor.

"Asyla!" Judge cried.

For a split second, Asyla had the grace to look embarrassed. Then that strange smile was back on her face. She said sarcastically, "Oh, no, have I been caught in the act?"

"What are you doing?" I asked, astounded.

"I was bored." Sweeping back her long hair, Asyla glared at Judge. "You invite us here for an entire weekend of events, and then you cancel everything.

Opening your presents seemed like a good way to kill time."

Before Judge or I could reply, Asyla dumped the box on the bed, leaped up, and rushed from the room.

The packages on the bed jostled together as the mattress bounced from her speedy departure. The large box tumbled toward the side of the bed.

"Stop!" I cried, shouting at the box as if it were a dog that could obey commands. The box fell to the hardwood floor with a surprising crash. A sudden powerful odor—like something you might smell in a doctor's office—stopped me in my tracks.

I looked at Judge in shock and said, "That smells like..."

"Scotch." She finished my sentence for me. "This box contains liquor."

"Hooch? Booze?" I asked and saw the corners of her mouth twitch in a little smile at my outburst. I couldn't resist trying to get her to smile more. I rambled off a few other slang names for liquor. "Giggle water? Bootleg? Moonshine? Coffin varnish? Firewater? Hair of the dog?"

"Yes, G. Codd, yes." I could see she was trying hard to smile. "And that means we now

SOME SLANG NAMES FOR LIQUOR

Hooch
Booze
Giggle water
Bootleg
Moonshine
Coffin varnish
Firewater
Hair of the dog
White lightning

have an illegal substance leaking all over my room. Grab some towels from my washbasin, please. We need to get this cleaned up."

"Who would give you a present like this for your engagement?" I asked, handing her the towels.

"I don't know. There's no card. But whoever gave it to me doesn't know me very well." And that was true. Judge would never be a part of anything that even hinted of illegality.

"Do you think this has something to do with John's disappearance?" I asked her.

"I'm not sure, but I hope not." She was quiet for a bit, soaking up the liquor. I could tell she was thinking things over. Finally, Judge said, "Grab that book from my nightstand, G. Codd. We can check if that second plane is one of ours."

I turned to pick up the book—and spotted Mang lurking in the doorway of the bedroom.

His eyes shone brightly above his long dark beard. "I knew I detected ze smell of something with ze nose!" he said in his strange accent.

"Yes," Judge said. "I was just going to see if the waters have calmed. I want to send someone to the mainland to alert the police."

Judge headed for the door.

In my study of illusions, I have seen magicians perform many acts. But none was as terrifying as the transformation that took place just then. In an instant, Mang's face twisted into a smirk of grim satisfaction, and he drew himself up to his full, powerful height.

In surprise, Judge took a protective step toward me.

June 13, 1925

Like a snake shedding his skin, we watched Mang ze Magnifico, Master of the Séance, drop his disguise. The man he truly was began to emerge.

He moved with deadly confidence now, closing the bedroom door and blocking it with his body. The man crossed his arms over his wide chest. Without a trace of an accent, he said, "No one is going anywhere."

Mang blocked the door!

Mang was a fraud!

June 13, 1925

10:15 PM

"I knew you weren't for real!" I cried. "You're a fraud, just as I said!"

Immediately, I realized he must have something to do with John's disappearance. Before Mang could even respond, I shouted, "Who are you? What have you done with John?"

"Keep your voice down, boy," Mang, or whoever he really was, hissed in a threatening tone. "I'll tell you all about John, more than you might want to know, but only if you take me to the other boxes like this one." He pointed one long finger at the broken box on the floor by the bed. "I must have what's inside them."

"You want the hooch?" I asked. At the same time, Judge said, "What other boxes? You can't keep us here!"

Mang gave her a smug smile. "I have more authority than you might think," he told her.

Judge laughed. "Whoever you are, you have the wrong idea. This box isn't even mine!"

But Mang ignored her. "You must lead me to the other boxes like this one."

This was getting annoying. I said, "You're not listening to us. We don't know about any boxes. Who are you?"

"That will be revealed to you shortly." Mang's whisper had a sharp edge. "Once I have what I came here for. "

Judge took a step toward him. "I demand to know who you are!"

June 13, 1925

The man's eyes turned to slits. "All right. We'll see if this makes a difference." Mang reached into his cape. Was he grabbing for a weapon?

I had to do something. "Wait!" I shouted. To my surprise, Mang stopped. He looked at me curiously, and I could see intelligence flashing behind his eyes. This man was not the fool he had pretended to be. I had to outsmart him somehow.

"Yes, boy?" he asked, one eyebrow arched. "I'm waiting. But what exactly am I waiting for?"

Maybe if we played along with him, I could get Mang out of the room. Then I could lock the door and pound on the walls for help—even climb out the window if I had to.

"Fine, all right." I let my shoulders slump as a sign of defeat. "Judge, you'd better take him to the boxes."

Dumbfounded, Judge gazed at me as if she thought I'd lost my mind.

Many illusionists claim that they have telepathic abilities.

January 4, 1925

Dear Master of Telepathy,

Harry Houdini told me you didn't learn my birthplace by using telepathy. When you went for a glass of water, you snuck to the public library next door! You used public records to find where I was born and returned saying you'd read my mind. Shame on you!

Sincerely,

Agnes Bernel

Houdini helped put a stop to this "library" trick!

They choose audience members and claim to communicate with them without speaking. I doubt that strangers can really accomplish such a feat. But I do believe that close friends and family, through years of shared experiences, develop their own secret language.

I stared at Judge and hoped she would understand the look on my face.

Please follow my lead. I think this might be our only chance.

It took only an instant. Her expression spoke back to me, *I trust you.*

Her entire body posture transformed as she decided to play along. She glared at me and yelled, "What are you doing, boy! You fool! You just gave us away." Judge took a breath and faced Mang. "All right. I'll take you to the boxes. Just don't bring the boy. I don't trust that he won't interfere."

Smart move. She was trying to get Mang to leave me alone in the room, which would give me a chance to find a way to get help.

Mang shook his head. "I can't do that. He might alert the wrong people."

"True." Judge bit her lower lip as if thinking of what to do. She gave me a quick glance—*Now it's your turn to trust me*—and looked back at Mang. "Then you'd better tie his hands and legs," she said. Other people might have felt betrayed by Judge for giving Mang such an idea. But other people do not have Houdini as their hero.

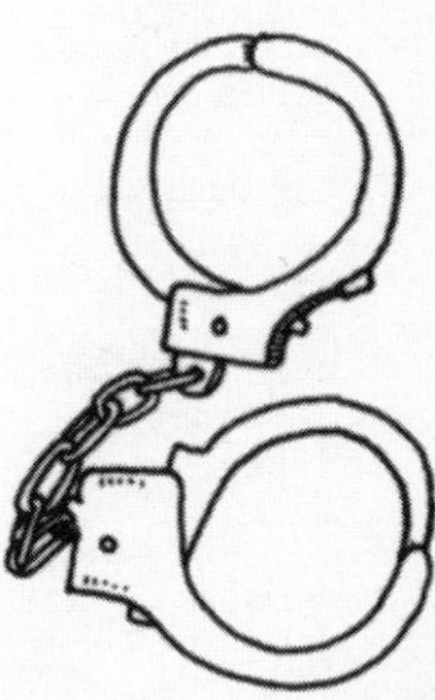

June 13, 1925

They can't escape ropes as easily as I can.

"Ropes...," Mang mused, nodding. Our plan was working!

"I have a better idea," Mang said and pulled out a pair of handcuffs from beneath his cape. Before I could protest, he sat me down and handcuffed my wrist to the leg of a heavy dresser.

"Yes," Mang said, testing the cuffs to make sure they were secure. "This will work nicely." Judge was speechless for a moment. Clearly, she had not planned on handcuffs. But she recovered and continued with our act. "Good idea," she said. "Let's go."

FIVE WAYS HOUDINI ESCAPES HANDCUFFS

1) Key: Often Houdini hides a key on himself to open the cuffs.

2) String: With older cuffs, Houdini can create a shoestring "lasso" to hook inside the lock and pull the bolt back.

3) Placement: Houdini has cuffs placed higher up on his arms—this looser fit allows him to simply slip off the cuffs.

4) Trick Cuffs: Houdini presses a secret lever on a pair of fake cuffs and they snap loose.

5) Bang: Some cuffs can be opened just by banging them—keyhole facing down—on a hard surface. Houdini sometimes hides a lead plate in his pant leg for this reason, but the heel of a shoe or the floor will do.

Mang leaned in close to me. "By the way, don't even think of shouting for help or banging on the wall. If I hear you doing either, I will be back. And I won't be happy. Come on, Miss Pinkerton, we have a date with a few boxes."

Judge shot me one final look. Her expression was easy to read: Good luck.

Mang and Judge left the room, closing the door behind them.

No problem, I thought, looking down at the handcuffs.

I could see at a glance the best way to open these cuffs. A good knock against a hard surface should snap them right open.

Unfortunately, the cuffs were hooked to my wrist and the dresser at an awkward angle. There wasn't any way for me to bang them against the floor with enough force.

Hurry up! I shouted at myself.

With my free hand, I reached down and took off one of my shoes. I brought the hard wooden heel down on the cuff around my wrist. There was a sharp jolt as part of the heel struck the bone of my arm.

But the metal handcuffs clattered to the floor, and just like that, I was free.

Judge! I have to help Judge!

I ran out into the hallway. I was opening my mouth to shout for help—but then I

remembered Mang's threat. If he heard me, things might get worse for both me and Judge.

I didn't know where Judge and Mang had gone. For all I knew they might be behind one of these doors. If I knocked on one, Mang might open it and recapture me!

Even Houdini might be stumped by this situation. I wasn't sure who I could turn to for help. Mr. Hatherford was too sick to disturb. Any of the other people in the mansion could be working with Mang.

I stood paralyzed in the center of the long hallway, unsure what to do next. On the bright side, it felt good to give the villain a face. If Mang was the bad guy, he must have been the one who kidnapped John—and probably the Scotsman, as well.

I examined the case in my head, looking for a thread that I could pull to unravel some of the mystery.

The Scotsman!

Yes, there was a thread I could really grab onto. I decided on a plan.

While part of my brain shouted at me to rush off and help Judge, I knew that was risky. Once I found them, what would I do? Mang was much bigger than I, and I couldn't overpower him.

I had to find the Scotsman!

I'd have to let Judge deal with Mang on her own. If anyone could handle the situation, it was she.

In the meantime, I would try to find the Scotsman. If I could discover what happened to him and locate him, he might be able to answer some of my questions.

The last time I had seen the Scotsman, he had been standing directly in front of me in the Great Hall. Our search party had not discovered anything in the room that showed us what might have happened to the man. But I had not been so desperate at that point. Maybe now I would see something I had missed earlier.

I rushed down the winding hallways and stairways until I finally reached the Great Hall. Rather than turn on the huge overhead lights and reveal my presence, I picked up a candelabra from the top of the grand staircase and lit the candles.

The room was now completely empty—the fires long dead.

I stood where I had interviewed the Scotsman. Once more, I replayed his disappearance and the moments after in my mind. The Scotsman standing in front of me...the power going off...darkness, confusion...Judge coming down the stairs...the search party...Asyla tossing a piece of paper that bounced off the back wall of a fireplace...

Wait! How could the paper have bounced off the back of the fireplace? They all had large, ornate screens to protect the rugs from sparks. The screens would have blocked the paper from striking the fireplace's top.

I turned to the fireplace that Asyla had been lounging near. The screen of the fireplace was placed off to the side. It looked like a giant, obvious exit. Could the Scotsman have climbed up the chimney?

The fire inside had long since gone dead. The fireplace was large enough for any number of people my size to fit into. I entered it and looked up. I saw immediately that there was no way the Scotsman had gone up the chimney. It was far too narrow.

I was wasting time! Judge could be in danger, and I was fumbling around in ashes!

Quickly, I examined the rest of the fireplace. I didn't see it at first. Then peering more closely, I made an amazing discovery.

A panel sat in the side wall of the fireplace. The panel had four tiles and looked like this:

Had I just uncovered a lock that somehow used the four elements, FIRE, EARTH, AIR, and WATER? There was only one way to find out.

I touched the FIRE tile, thinking it might be the key to open the lock. After all, I was standing in a fireplace. The FIRE tile felt a little loose and jiggled a bit, but nothing happened. I pressed harder, but still nothing. Going down the line, I pressed each of the tiles and got the same response: zero.

The rumrunner had put these tiles of the elements here for a reason.

What would be the most important element to a rumrunner? I thought of things that would be important to a bootlegger, and thought of the names I had rattled off to Judge earlier, trying to get her to smile: Booze, hair of the dog, firewater, hooch...

And then I had the key!

The solution was to press two tiles at the same time to create an element crucial to any rumrunner:

FIREWATER.

A slang word for liquor. I held my breath, reached out and pressed the two tiles FIRE and WATER.

With a soft whoosh, the inside wall of the fireplace swung open. I had done it!

Through the door made of brick, I saw only darkness. I grabbed a fireplace poker. My mother didn't raise a fool—I wasn't going to end up trapped again. I lay the poker on the floor across the doorway. If it started to shut behind me, the door wouldn't be able to completely close.

Grabbing the candelabra with five lit candles, I stepped through the door and into yet another secret passageway. Unlike the last one I had discovered, this passageway had a straight line of stairs that led down. In the dim

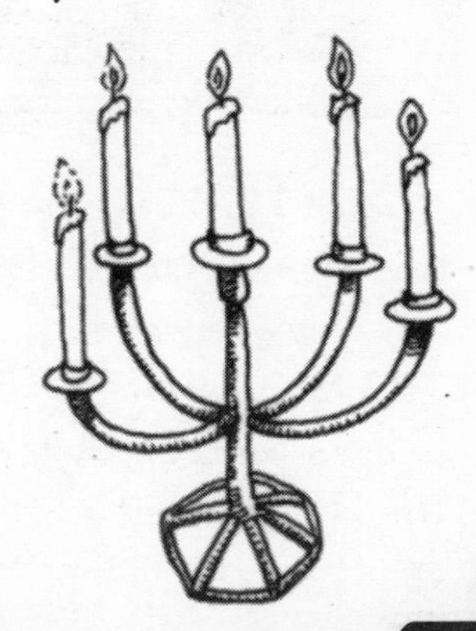

light of the candles, I could make out at least two sets of footprints leading down the stairs.

Just as I thought, after I was two or three steps in, I heard a banging sound. The door had started to close, but the poker blocked its path.

At the bottom of the staircase, I found myself in what appeared to be the entrance to a dungeon. It was a circular chamber the size of a small cottage. Dangling from the low ceiling, ancient pipes that must have carried sewage or water at one time wound here and there. Six vaulted tunnels of decaying brick sprouted from the chamber like rotting branches of a tree. Etched numbers, one through six, had been carved over the opening of each tunnel. One more legacy of the rumrunner who had built the mansion.

Which tunnel should I take? I looked more closely at the floor. The candlelight allowed me to see several feet down each tunnel, and I could see tracks in several of them.

But there was only one obvious choice. I rushed down tunnel #4, holding the candelabra in front of me. The tracks in this tunnel were the only ones that led away from the chamber.

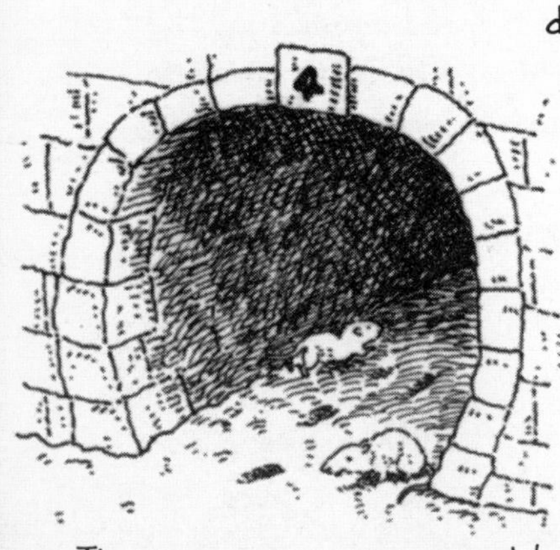

There were rats in the tunnels!

I felt like I was racing the circle of light formed by the candles—and winning. My feet came down on damp

June 13, 1925

HOW TO BE LIKE HARRY HOUDINI BRICK WALL TRICK

1) A sheet is placed onstage, covering a trapdoor. Bricklayers build a brick wall on top of the sheet.
2) Audience members inspect the wall for hidden doors.
3) Screens are placed on either side of the wall.
4) Go behind one screen.
5) Your assistant under the stage should now open the trapdoor. This trapdoor will allow you to squeeze under the wall without the audience knowing.
6) Emerge on the other side of the wall and amaze the audience!

objects that first squished and then crunched. I refused to consider what they might be. Several terrified rats squeaked in panic as they fled into dark holes.

The tunnel took several sharp turns as I followed the tracks—and then I nearly smacked into a mold-covered wall.

It was a dead end.

No! I shouted inside my head. I must have taken the wrong tunnel and wasted precious time. But this is where the tracks had led.

I took a breath and had a closer look. A brick wall might appear to be the end of the line to most people. But when looked at through Houdini's eyes, a wall was another wonderful setup for an illusion.

Because I was looking for it, the steel ring concealed in the ground was almost instantly clear. Getting a good grip on this handle, I pulled. The brick tunnels echoed with the screeching sound of the ancient hinges. A trapdoor in the floor swung open.

Holding the candelabra down into the opening, I saw part of a small circular tunnel that was about three feet in diameter. It dipped down on this side of the wall and straightened out. I could just barely make out where the passage rose back up on the other side of the wall.

There were drag marks in the small passage, and they looked fresh. The Scotsman or even Judge could be on the other side. I would have to go in. The candelabra would be too awkward to carry, so I set it on the ground and removed a single candle. This would have to be enough light.

The trapdoor

I lowered myself through the trapdoor, feeling like I was crawling into the mouth of a hungry lion.

If I crouched very low, I could make my way without having to crawl or rub my head against the slimy top of the tunnel. After only a few feet, the passage curved up and led to an open trapdoor.

As I climbed into what appeared to be a small chamber carved into rock, my shirt caught on the locking mechanism of the trapdoor. The door leaned back against the brick wall I had just passed under. A pipe that ran along the wall had drooped over the years, coming to rest on top of the trapdoor.

June 13, 1925

Two boxes sat immediately in front of me. Bringing he candle closer, I jiggled them and heard the istinctive clink of glass against glass. I didn't need to mell it to know what the boxes contained. It was a idden stash of liquor, and the lack of dust on the boxes et me know they had been put there recently.

I took a step further into the hidden chamber. My mall candle was the only source of light. The back wall f the room, if there was one, remained hidden in the itch black.

Just then, I heard the sound of breathing.

"Hello...?" I whispered, but inside my head, I creamed, Run!

There was silence and then, above the sound of my ounding heart, I could hear the breathing again. It sounded agged, and I realized someone might be in trouble.

Another step, and another, and the candlelight slid long the ground...over a shoe and then a second hoe...and before long, I was looking at the Scotsman.

I gasped.

He lay face up, but a blindfold covered his eyes and a ag prevented him from speaking. I saw his chest rising nd lowering, and realized the sounds of breathing didn't natch with his. They were coming from further inside he room. I took two more steps and...there was John.

Jumpin' John Hatherford, Judge's fiancé, the man we ad all been searching for, right here in front of me. He y awkwardly on his side, as if someone had tossed him here. He was the source of the ragged breathing.

"John?" I said. "Can you hear me?" I brought the andle down to examine his face. His closed eyes

fluttered slightly, but beyond that, his pale skin showed little signs of life.

I needed to get help. "John, I'm going to get a doctor. I'll be right back."

I turned to leave the small chamber—

Behind me, quick footsteps rushed out of the darkness. Before I could turn around to see who was approaching, I was grabbed roughly from behind. A large arm pinned my arms against the sides of my body, and a blindfold slid over my head.

"Let me go, Mang!" I shouted, wriggling in the strong man's grasp.

"Don't move!" a voice hissed in a husky whisper. It was a man, that much I was sure of. "I'm going to tie you up. If you struggle..."

My assailant didn't finish his sentence. He didn't need to.

The man gave me a push, indicating I should sit down on the damp floor. I felt the ends of the rope brush against me. And I was suddenly more thankful for all my hours practicing to be an illusionist than ever before.

Breath on my cheek and then the voice was whispering in my ear again. "Not to worry. You can't see it now, but I'll leave your candle up on the wall. After we land, I will let people know you are down here."

After we land? This must be the owner of the second airplane.

June 13, 1925

I heard the shuffle of footsteps and grunting as if heavy objects were being moved—and then the trapdoor closed as my assailant left the chamber. Seconds later, a strange vibrating noise filled the room. POP! A sharp hissing was followed by the sound of running water, as if someone had just opened a large faucet all the way.

I remembered that the trapdoor had been supporting an ancient pipe. That support was removed when my assailant closed the door—and the pipe must have ruptured. Then I felt a small pool of cold liquid spread out around me.

There was no doubt: the room was filling up with water!

TEC TIP

HOUDINI'S ADVICE FOR ESCAPING FROM ROPE BINDINGS.

First: Be tied standing up.

Second: While being tied, swell the muscles, expand the chest, slightly hunch the shoulders, and hold the arms a little away from the sides.

Third: Wear a coat or other extra clothing while being tied to improve the slack.

It was sloshing over my legs by the time I escaped the ropes and tore off my blindfold. I had to get John and the Scotsman out of here, or they would drown! But as my eyes focused in the dim light of the candle, I could see instantly that they were gone—and so were the boxes of liquor.

Mang must have dragged everything out with him!

I climbed to my feet as water from the ruptured pipe continued to pour into the small room. It had nearly reached my chest when I dove under it and reached for the handle of the trapdoor.

I managed to find the steel ring and pulled. But it wouldn't budge. The locking mechanism must have clicked into place when my assailant closed the door. Unable to hold my breath any longer, I rose back to the surface only to discover the water had reached the level of my mouth and was getting closer to the flame of the candle. Unless I found a way out of here, the candle wouldn't be the only thing to be extinguished.

My hands worked quickly but calmly under my jacket, and tore at the lining. The fabric gave way and I grabbed the lock kit I always kept hidden there.

I swam back down below the surface, knowing that I only had one chance. By the time I ran out of breath and tried to go back up, the water would have reached the ceiling. But I can do this blindfolded, I thought, and it's a good thing, because suddenly the dim light of the candle was gone. The water must have put out the flame.

I worked fast and in complete darkness. The steel pick slipped, and I almost dropped it—something that would have had fatal results. My lungs burned, bright spots exploded behind my eyes, and my limbs began to feel like they belonged to someone else. Still my fingers continued to work. The tool twisted in the keyhole. Finally, I heard a wonderful CLICK!

I yanked on the handle and the trapdoor opened slowly. I swam through the small tunnel and banged my head against the trapdoor on the other side.

TEC TIP

In his book, Houdini recommends that magicians carry a wire. This "lock pick" can be shaped and formed to meet the needs of different locks. It works especially well on older locks!

June 13, 1925

I had to get out! My feet managed to grip the slippery rock. With all my might I pushed against the trapdoor. Like a cork exploding from a bottle, I popped out of the tunnel, and the swirling water pushed me skittering across the dark passageway—

In a blur, I saw Judge's face. She was holding a lantern in one hand.

I had just a second to think, What's she doing here? when a hand wrapped around my ankle and pulled.

Never letting go of my ankle, Judge stumbled backward and banged into the wall but remained standing. I slid across the floor on my belly, out of the rushing stream of water, and came to rest at her feet.

I stared up at her face, gasping for air. She moved the lantern closer to get a better look at me. "G. Codd, are you okay?" Her voice was thick with worry. "Talk to me!"

For a moment, I was too stunned to speak and spluttered for air. "How did you find me?" I finally asked between periods of sucking air into my still-burning lungs. "How did you get away from Mang?"

Judge helped me to my feet. "I'll answer all of your questions later. But right now..."

"Right now," I said, finishing her sentence, "the bad guy is headed for the second airplane. We have to stop him!"

The storm had passed.

June 14, 1925

3:40 AM

As Judge and I ran through the dark tunnels beneath the Hatherford mansion, I filled her in on my adventures in the hidden room. I quickly told her about discovering John and the Scotsman. Judge listened but didn't ask any questions. She must be in too much shock, I thought.

With Judge carrying her lantern, we sprinted up the stone stairway to the inside of the fireplace. The poker had prevented the door from locking shut.

"That was good thinking, G. Codd," Judge said, indicating the poker as we hurried past it and into the Great Hall. "Not only did it keep you from getting locked inside, it was the clue that told me where you had gone."

We rushed out of the double doors of the Great Hall and began to make our way around the side of the mansion. The storm had finally traveled out to sea, and the sky was full of glittering stars. My dripping clothes soaked up the cool night air and sent shivers down my spine.

"Wait!" I cried, stopping. "Shouldn't we bring weapons? You never know what we might find!"

"I think I know what we'll discover," Judge called over her shoulder. I sprinted to catch up with her. She continued, "Besides, weapons like guns or knives are for fools, G. Codd. Your brain is the greatest weapon you have."

Even in this crazy, frantic situation, Judge's words

triggered memories in my head. I replayed her soothing advice about Occam's razor, her confidence that I was skilled enough to handle the crime scene, her ability to track me through the underground passages...

Bizarre timing, but suddenly one of my life's mysteries became clear to me. "Now I know...," I said.

"What?" Judge asked, as we continued to run. "What do you know?"

"I know why you have the nickname Judge."

She glanced at me and gave me a quick smile. But this was no time to philosophize. Just as we reached the edge of the hidden airstrip, the silence of the night was shattered by a loud coughing sound. An engine was starting up.

The second airplane was rolling out onto the airstrip. In order to take off, it would have to get past us.

"No, you don't," Judge said quietly and stepped in front of the airplane.

The airplane made no signs of slowing. The propeller's blades spun like giant chopping knives. But Judge did not move.

Without hesitating, I stepped next to Judge.

"G. Codd, get back!" Judge shouted. Neither of us moved, however. We stood our ground as the hulking piece of machinery lumbered toward us.

Like any magician, I held up both my hands so the pilot of the plane could see them.

"Nothing here," I said, even though I knew I couldn't be heard above the roar of the engine. I waved my right hand to show it was empty. "And nothing here," I said, waving my empty left hand. "Ohhhh, but what's this?"

June 14, 1925

With a quick sleight of hand, I produced a small metal rod in my right hand. I held it over my head to be sure the pilot could see it.

My performance had the desired effect and was much more satisfying than any standing ovation would ever be. The plane came to an almost immediate stop, and its engines shut down.

"You're too much, G. Codd," Judge said.

Earlier, after Judge and I had first discovered this second craft, I had returned to the airplane and removed the metal rod from the rudder. I assumed it must perform an important function.

"No matter what happens," Judge told me as the propeller wound down, "I want you to know how proud I am of you...."

The door to the cockpit opened and the pilot jumped out.

June 14, 1925

I guess I shouldn't have been surprised, but I was. The pilot was John Hatherford. Judge's fiancé.

Through the open door, I could see the Scotsman waving happily from the passenger seat. He shouted at me, "See you at the nixt poppet shew!" John closed the door, blocking the Scotsman from view.

"Darling," John said to Judge. He had a sad puppy dog look on his face. "I don't know what to say."

Judge was frozen, her eyes wide, her mouth clamped shut.

John turned to me. "Hello, G. Codd, old pal. On the case as always, I see. Can I have my airplane part now? I'll need that if I want to survive more than five seconds in the air."

"No," Judge said in a faraway voice. "I want the truth out of you, John. What is happening here?" Her voice rose. "And if you lie, I swear I'll make your life very, very difficult."

John must have realized the puppy dog look wasn't working. He replaced it with the lopsided grin that I had practiced so many times in the mirror.

"I bet you've figured it out by now," he said to Judge.

"He's smuggling liquor," I said. "He's a bootlegger."

John's grin dipped. "That's not exactly true, pal. I was a bootlegger. It's all over now. As of this weekend. This is the last run."

"Let me guess, John," Judge said as she took a step toward him. "You were doing it all for me, right?"

John's grin grew back to full force. "That's right, darling."

"Stop it!" Judge snapped. "Stop calling me darling."

Watching John's face was like watching a person flip

through the pages of a picture book. Different expressions flashed by until John settled on one. He must have assumed it made him look like a tough protector. "Fine, Justine," he said. "But it was all for you—"

I blew out air in frustration. This was getting us nowhere, and just hurting Judge more.

I took a step forward. "How did you do it?"

John was too busy trying to gaze into Judge's eyes to bother with my question.

"Answer him, John!" Judge glared at him. "How was the operation set up? Answer him, or I'll scream so loud this field will be filled with people in no time."

"Do I get my part back if I do?" When Judge ignored his request, John sighed. "Locals made the liquor and traveled by boat to the island. They left the booze

hidden in the cellar. I would pick it up and deliver it around the country. It normally went like clockwork. But the other night, the boxes of booze got mixed up with our engagement presents."

Judge cried, "You made deliveries in our airplanes?"

"Well, yes, of course," John answered, as if that were a dumb question. "You have no idea how thrilling it's been."

"I was so proud of our air courier business," Judge said. "You were just using it as a cover! You were using me! I helped you run a smuggling ring, and I didn't even know it!"

Things were starting to come together in my mind. "You had Judge arrange deliveries," I said to John. "Deliveries to people like Virgil Gates."

"Right again, pal," John said. "I would drop off crates of hooch to Virgil in Chicago. He would sell it to local speakeasies there. Virgil made the delivery easy this weekend by coming here."

John was on a roll, and I wanted to keep him talking. "And the Scotsman?"

"I hired him and instructed him to meet me back here before the party

John hid the liquor in the cello

last night." John sounded proud of himself. "I told the Scotsman I needed him to broadcast a puppet show for a children's party. He jumped at the chance—it's not like his idea for this thing called television will ever amount to anything! While you were all inside, I wheeled JENNY onto the airstrip outside the Great Hall. At the same time, the Scotsman installed his equipment. I made him believe that I wanted the children to think it was magic, so he must remain unseen."

"His broadcast was just a diversion?" I asked, but knew the answer.

"Yes, that was the plan," John replied. "Everyone thought they saw my plane land outside the Great Hall. When the crowd rushed out the door, I darted through the empty house gathering evidence that the police might be able to use against us."

Judge gave a sharp bark of laughter. "Us? Who is US?"

"Why, you and me, dar—Justine," John said. "I didn't do this for the money. I did it for the thrill. We always talked about living on the edge. And look at us! I'd call this pretty exciting, wouldn't you?"

"Crazy is a better word," I offered.

John kept his eyes on Judge, ignoring me again. "Now, Justine. Think about it. You never would have known about any of this if the Scotsman had not gotten lost twice and wandered around the mansion. If that storm hadn't grounded me for so long, I would've snatched up all the incriminating evidence and carried it off without anyone being the wiser. I'd still be your John and you would still be my darling."

There was silence. I imagined the thoughts that must

be flying around in Judge's head. Was she thinking of taking him back? I tried breaking the moment by pointing out more of John's misdeeds. "You're the one who turned off the power and nabbed the Scotsman."

John sighed and rolled his eyes as if I was being nitpicky. "I couldn't let him tell you about my involvement. I listened as you interviewed him from behind the secret door in the fireplace. When I heard you get too close to the truth, I shut off the power and brought him down into the tunnels. I tied him up and said he had to pretend to be unconscious. But I told him it was all part of the game."

I shot him a stony look. "I didn't think it was a game when you left me tied up in that dungeon and I almost drowned!"

"I'm sorry about that, pal," John said. "I heard you open the trapdoor to the secret room. I had to make you think I was a victim, so I lay down next to the Scotsman."

"And then you tied me up!" I was furious.

John looked at his hands. "Like I told you, I was going to let people know where you were when I landed. Justine, what do you say?"

Judge hesitated. Then her eyes narrowed and she took another step toward John. "This was supposed to be the happiest time of my life. This was a party for US! For our future! You used me, you used our engagement. There is no future for us!"

"You don't mean that," John said. "I had to do what I did this weekend. My contacts in different cities told me that someone was asking questions about our operation. I knew the police were onto us. I was afraid I might be

Judge wasn't having any of it.

arrested at any time. The crowd of guests at the party offered the perfect distraction for me to get the evidence out of the house." Judge remained stone-faced, and John tried a different approach. "Think of what breaking our engagement would do to my poor old father. It would kill him. Do you want that on your shoulders?"

John reached out to touch her arm.

Judge jumped back as if recoiling from a snake. "Stay away from me. You are disgusting! You can't blackmail me into loving you. You made your father think that you might be dead!"

"I am sorry about that. I love my old man."

"You seem to be sorry about a lot," I observed.

"I loved you," Judge said. "Why didn't you just talk to me?"

John acted like he didn't hear her. "I planned to return here tomorrow. I was going stumble out of the woods and say, 'Golly, what happened? I guess I bumped my head while landing the airplane in the storm.'"

Judge said, "That way your father would never know you were a criminal and would still give you his money."

I added, "And you could claim the glory of being the first person to fly solo across the Atlantic."

"Well...no. I wasn't going to do that," John said. But it was clear from his hesitation that this is exactly what he meant to do. Maybe he wasn't such a good actor after all.

"Liar!" I shouted. "You were never going to give this up. This was just a way to trick the police for now. You were going to keep on bootlegging."

I could see I had hit on the truth. John's face flashed with rage. "Boys shouldn't play grown-up games. Boys who do that might get hurt."

Drawing herself up to her full height, Judge pointed at John like a goddess from a mount. "Don't you dare threaten him!"

John flipped through expressions and landed on the hurt puppy dog again. "I'm sorry. Honest. Justine, you have to let me go. I really do have to act right now. The police are closer than we think."

She crossed her arms. "Oh, I know for a fact that they are."

"That's why I need to leave

Judge wouldn't stand for any threats!

right now! I have all the evidence of the operation on the plane. I'll destroy it, and then it will be their word against ours. If you stand by me, we can't lose. Everyone knows you're one of the most honest people—"

Judge glared at him. "I put off my dreams of going to law school to run your delivery business!"

"Women don't belong in law school and you—" John took a deep breath. "Justine. Don't be silly. Think of us. Think of our life together!"

"Some life," I said. "You were about to run her over with the plane to get out of here."

John threw up his hands. "Justine, are you going to listen to a child or to your heart?"

"They're both saying the same thing," she said, gazing back at him. It was as if she were searching for something in his eyes.

There was suddenly the feeling that we were teetering on the edge of a cliff. The world stood still and everything seemed hushed, as if waiting for the next moment.

Without breaking eye contact with John, Judge raised her voice slightly and said, "Mr. Ness, you can come out now. I think we have all we need."

Mr. Ness? Who was Mr. Ness?

Panic spread across John's face. "Justine, what are you doing?"

"Don't move!" A voice called. And for the second time since I met him, Mang the Magnifico emerged from the shadows. He was reaching beneath his cape with one hand and tugging at his long beard with the other.

"No!" I shouted, and took up my defensive stance.

June 14, 1925

"Relax, G. Codd! He's on our side," Judge spoke quickly. "I'd like you to meet Mr. Eliot Ness."

Mr. Who? I thought. The man I knew as Mang was holding a badge in one hand and his long fake beard in the other.

UNIVERSITY OF CHICAGO YEARBOOK, 1925

Voted most likely to make arrests...

ELIOT NESS

This 22-year-old Chicago-born graduate earned a degree in business and law. You might have seen him around campus practicing jujitsu or quietly reading a book. Ness says he plans to work on a case down South this summer, pursuing "interesting leads." In the fall, he'll return to school to study criminology and work at the Prohibition Bureau. Ness says, who knows? He might just join the Justice Department and go after the big crooks like Al Capone. (Yeah, right. That's just an untouchable dream!)

It wasn't until later that I realized Mang was an anagram for G-man, which is a nickname for "Government man."

June 14, 1925

Eliot Ness

Ness showed me the badge he had taken from beneath his cape. "I've been working undercover as Mang the Magnifico to break the smuggling ring."

Seeing I still wasn't convinced, Judge put a hand on my shoulder. "Mr. Ness is the one who was following us in the parlor's secret passage—"

Ness nodded. "I thought Miss Pinkerton might be meeting John in there. When I saw it was you, G. Codd, I turned back."

"After we left you handcuffed in my room," Judge said to me, "I convinced Mr. Ness that we were on the side of the good guys. He told me that he wasn't really Mang, but a federal agent. So I came up with this plan. We would get John to confess in front of hidden witnesses what he's been up to all these months—"

I guess John was convinced of Mr. Ness's true identity. Because he turned and started to run toward the nearby woods before Mr. Ness could handcuff him. But John was stopped dead in his tracks by yet another figure who stepped out of the shadows.

"Pop," John said, skittering to a stop in the wet grass. "Pop..."

It was Hiram Hatherford. John stood before his father, and now the guilty little boy routine didn't look like an act.

"You heard me? You heard what I said, Pop?" John pleaded with his father. "I did this...I did this because I love you..."

Mr. Hatherford looked like this ordeal had stolen the remains of his youth. With tears in eyes, he spoke quietly. "John. Shhh. Please. Don't say anything more." He shook his white head. "You betrayed me. You betrayed our family. I tried to give you everything in the world, but the one thing that I don't seem to have given you is a sense of right and wrong."

Mr. Hatherford took a deep breath and stepped away from his son. "Well, I have the feeling you're about to have plenty of time to learn that lesson. Arrest him!"

His father's words must have frozen John with shame. He remained unmoving as Mr. Ness placed the handcuffs on him.

With a wink at me, Mr. Ness said, "Let's hope these handcuffs work a little better on the real bad guys."

Judge moved quickly to Mr. Hatherford, who was trembling violently, and put a comforting hand on his shoulder. She signaled to the nurse who had been standing nearby to join us. I overheard Judge ask the nurse to take Mr. Hatherford to his room.

Eliot Ness started to lead John back to the mansion. Questions whirled in my head. I called, "Mr. Ness, how did you know about John? Why were you working here?"

Holding tightly to one of John's arms, Mr. Ness paused and turned to me. "Eight months ago, crates of liquor were found washed up along the coast—near the spot where John's first plane crashed." He tapped his forehead. "I put two and two together. The crates came

June 14, 1925

Crates of liquor washed up on the shore.

from John's plane. No one else would come after a man with so much wealth and power, but what do I have to lose? Sorry about scaring you before in Miss Pinkerton's room, kid. I didn't want to blow my cover until I was sure I had the real bad guys." Mr. Ness waited a second and then added with a gleam in his eyes. "I came here seeking spirits as Mang ze Magnifico and I found them as Eliot Ness."

There was no sound. Only crickets.

"Okay, bad joke," Mr. Ness said quickly. "Anyway, John here can join his good pal Virgil Gates, who is already cuffed inside the mansion. They can wait for the local authorities to arrive together."

"What about Virgil's girlfriend, Asyla Notabe?" I asked.

Mr. Ness shrugged. "Interesting woman. I'd love to talk to her, but she's gone."

June 14, 1925

This caught me by surprise. "Gone? You mean vanished?"

"Not exactly," Mr. Ness said. "There was a dinghy at the dock. It's not there anymore. I don't know if Asyla had enough of this party or smelled trouble brewing. Either way, she's left the island."

"Are you going to send police after her?"

"Why? I have no evidence that she was involved in the bootlegging operation," Mr. Ness said.

Just then Judge walked over. "Can I have a moment with John, Mr. Ness?"

After a second's hesitation, Mr. Ness let go of John's arm and stepped a few feet away. For a long moment, Judge just stared at John. Finally, she said, "John, you cannot bend the law for your own enjoyment or personal gain. It doesn't bend, it only breaks. The same is true of a relationship. There are laws that must be obeyed in love—or it shatters. And then it's gone forever."

Judge turned away and walked over to the plane.

John's face cleared, and it was as if I were seeing him for the first time. There were no more masks. "Goodbye, Justine," he said quietly. But I don't know if she heard him. Then Ness was pulling him away, back toward the mansion.

Judge stood alone next to John's aircraft. She traced her fingers along the side, as if dreaming of where the future might have taken her.

June 14, 1925

I walked slowly over to her. "You know, I've changed my mind," I said after a few moments of silence. "I think people can see the future. You want to know what I see?"

Judge didn't answer me. I knew she was struggling with her emotions.

I looked directly at her. "I see a woman who's going to get what she wants out of life."

Judge let out a small sob. "Thank you, my friend," she whispered.

Judge looped an arm around my shoulders and we headed back to the house. The first rays of the sun were breaking over the horizon, casting our long shadows across the wet green grass and spreading bright light across the crystal-clear sky.

WARNING: This letter reveals the story's ending!

A NOTE FROM THE AUTHOR

One of the best parts about reading a good mystery is that you're never sure what's going to happen next. You get to imagine different paths the story might take. Will the hero dive into the pool of alligators or swing over them on a vine?

When I write, I do kind of the same thing. No, I don't swoo over a pool filled with snapping gators. But I do dream up new, imagined paths for people and events from history.

For example, Eliot Ness appears in NABBED! Ness was a famous crime fighter who brought down Al Capone, one of the biggest gangsters. But did Ness dress up like Mang ze Magnifico and crack a rum-smuggling ring in North Carolina right after college as he did in this story? Probably not.

While I tried to be true to the investigative techniques of 1925, my main goal was to write an exciting mystery. The mansion, Judge, even the island—they all seem real to me and, hopefully, to you. But remember, they're inventions c my imagination.

I hope you had fun reading NABBED!—just don't use G. Codd's journal as study material for your next history tes Or that pool of gators might look pretty good compared to your teacher's reaction.

Yours in time,

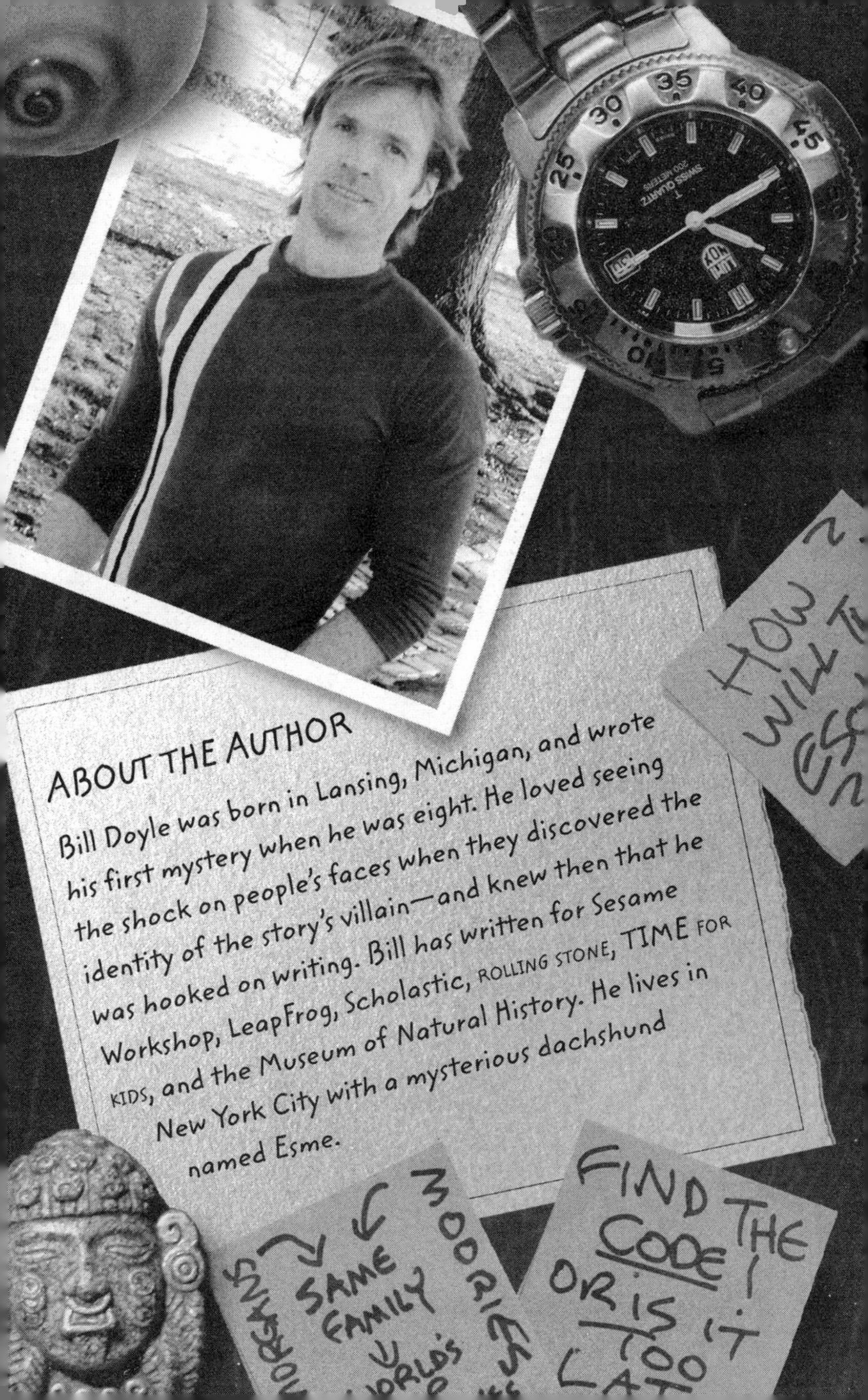

ABOUT THE AUTHOR

Bill Doyle was born in Lansing, Michigan, and wrote his first mystery when he was eight. He loved seeing the shock on people's faces when they discovered the identity of the story's villain—and knew then that he was hooked on writing. Bill has written for Sesame Workshop, LeapFrog, Scholastic, ROLLING STONE, TIME FOR KIDS, and the Museum of Natural History. He lives in New York City with a mysterious dachshund named Esme.

Check out these other gripping Crime Through Time™ books!

Now in stores!

Coming in July 2006!

Coming in July 2006!

And watch out for ICED! and TRAPPED!, coming in Fall 2006!